To Steal from the Dead
By Peter Barski
ISBN: 978-1-8380464-8-4

Published By: -

i2i
PUBLISHING

i2i Publishing. Manchester.

www.i2ipublishing.co.uk

Acknowledgements

I would like to thank Lionel Ross, the publisher at i2iPublishing.co.uk for agreeing to publish the book. I would also like to thank Mark Cripps, the Senior Editor at i2i Publishing, for his help in getting the book ready for publication. Finally, I would like to acknowledge my dear friend Ken Brevett for his moral support and encouragement.

Chapter 1

Comfort Foo

Great, I thought sarcastically, as I stared at the computer screen. Only thirty more days to complete my ongoing educational requirements. Then, I could renew my pharmacist licence. Having two years to get this accomplished, I did what most other people did; waited until the last minute and then scrambled into action. Procrastination, it's just human nature. The fact is I had been preoccupied with trying to salvage a relationship that came to nothing other than its ultimate demise. So, this last-minute distraction was a welcome occupation of my spare time, and a necessary one to keep my licence in good standing. This kept me driven, despite the drab nature of the course, The Opioid Epidemic in which there were several pages comparing the potencies of drugs available on the market today. These ranged from codeine, all the way up to fentanyl, the latter being the most potent. Morphine was the 'gold standard' and used as a measuring stick to rank the various pain medications' potencies.

Many of these drugs I would see prescribed daily, such as oxycodone and hydromorphone. They helped fuel the opioid epidemic which seemed to erupt sometime after the great recession of 2008. Pain clinics began springing up all over the country, and my home state of Florida became a beehive for them. People would drive here from as far as Tennessee to get prescriptions.

Oxycontin gained notoriety, as it contained large amounts of oxycodone. The tablets could be crushed, then snorted or injected, which also led to an epidemic of drug overdoses. The manufacturer eventually came up with a reformulation of the tablet which intertwined the active product with a long acting delivery vehicle made of wax to prevent this problem. But addicts could be quite crafty though when they need to be and many soon figured out how to separate the oxycodone from the gelatin wax by melting the tablets in microwaves.

Dilaudid was also a favorite among addicts. A young lady once told me that she cried the very first time she used it. She was in recovery when I had met her, but she used to inject drugs when she was using. She said it was like someone had wrapped her entire body in a warm, comfortable blanket.

It takes a lot of 'sand' to be an intravenous drug user. You had to crush the tablet into powder, place it in a spoon with preferably, some sterile water, boil it, and then draw it up into a needle and syringe. Then, you had to constrict the area above the injection site, find a suitable vein, and inject. Not everyone was cut out for it. It would turn into a ritual, counting your tablets, holding them, knowing you have enough of them for the here and now, but of course, using more than you had planned, leading to a sense of desperation and panic, later on; a vicious cycle that got worse and worse.

All of this was not directly touched on by the course I was studying, but was indirectly understood by me, given my occupation as a retail pharmacist. Next, the course referred to fentanyl, a very powerful synthetic opiate that was gaining notoriety. People were synthesizing it in home laboratories and dealers were using it as a cutting agent in heroin to add potency to it. To my amazement, the next screen showed the six chemicals needed to synthesize it, and the total cost of the combined ingredients, all obtainable for under four hundred dollars. These were NPP, sodium borohydride, propionyl chloride, THF and aniline. Molecular sieve was also used to bind some of the chemicals together. A four-hundred-dollar investment yielded eighteen grams of fentanyl with a street value of eighteen thousand dollars. I was amazed by this, and being curious, snapped a picture of the screen with my phone.

'I wonder how difficult it could be to make?', I thought. 'I'm certainly no Walter White, but if other people are making it from home, why couldn't I?' I wanted to do some research into this as soon as I got the damn course requirements done with.

It then occurred to me that I was contemplating doing something totally illegal. What had prompted me to even think about doing something like that? It certainly made no sense whatsoever given my rather esteemed occupation; one shrouded in trust. I could not think of any circumstance where a pharmacist had been reprimanded or convicted for making illegal drugs, unless of course they were never caught. But what would prompt me to even consider it? It was either out of boredom or the fact that I wanted to get my mind off my failed relationship, and that would be a good distraction. But to make and sell something illegally? Perhaps, the idea brought me back to my youth when I was in high school selling small amounts of pot to my fellow classmates. It had felt good. I remembered, being sought out by a popular high schooler to provide him with "herb" for an upcoming weekend party. I had even gone as far as growing several plants on the back porch of my parent's home, telling them they were tomato plants for a science project. Then one afternoon, my father was proudly showing a couple of his friends my plants when they promptly informed him that they were marijuana plants. That ended my career as a dope dealer rather quickly. Perhaps now that I was older and wiser, I could be more successful at an illegal undertaking?

I was startled to hear a knock on my front door, given it was evening time. Feeling somewhat guilty, I downsized my screen on the computer and then went out into the living room to see who was there. Opening it up, I found my friend Steve there with a bottle of Jack Daniels in his hand.

"Hey buddy," he gleamed. "I've come to see how you are doing, and I brought something to help numb you up." He lifted the bottle and smiled.

"Come on in bud," I said, inviting him in.

He walked in and I closed the door. He waited for me just inside, and then followed me to the dining room table, where he pulled out a chair and sat down. I went around the corner and got two glasses from the kitchen and then joined him. He poured us both a drink and then placed the bottle between us on the table.

"So, have you heard from Tricia?" he asked.

"Not for a couple of weeks now," I replied. "It's weird living only a few miles away and yet not seeing her."

"Yeah, but you'll be moving soon enough. When do you move into your new place?" he asked. We each took a sip of whiskey.

"In two weeks," I exclaimed. "It'll be nice to be much closer to work and much further from her!"

"Fuck that bitch! She really did a number on you. And to think you were commuting over an hour to and from work every day just to be near her. What a joke. My hat's off to you," he exclaimed, raising his glass.

I had been working in Fort Pierce for some time when I started dating Tricia. As our relationship evolved, I rented a house in Wellington, just to be near her. We had become close, but I was spending over eight hours a week driving to and from work, and it was exhausting me. The subject was a sour one between us, and she eventually decided to end things.

"I'm sure she didn't appreciate your sacrifices," he continued. "Then, she decides to break things off because why, she wasn't ready to settle down? She is over forty for crying out loud. What the fuck is her problem?"

"She said that she was in a dull and drab marriage for fifteen years and she wanted to explore more of what life had to offer her. Sounded like a crock of shit to me, but whatever," I tried to explain. I took a long sip and then poured myself some more.

"Oh sure, yet she sees you for over two years and lets you fall in love. That makes no sense." He looked puzzled as he drank.

I exclaimed, "Well here's to the feeling of being 'trapped'" and we both drained our glasses. He poured us each another whiskey and I began to feel warm inside my stomach.

"You know what helps me get over a nasty break up?" he asked me. "Listening to some very loud rock and roll music."

"I agree. I've been listening to the *Foo Fighters* while driving to work in the mornings," I told him.

"Oh man, great band!" he agreed.

"Yeah man. There are these two songs back-to-back on the *In Your Honor* CD, *The Last Song* and *Free Me* that I blare in the truck whenever my mind wanders off to her. It helps me get a grip and realise that it's over between us."

Leaning forward intently, Steve's eyes twinkled with excitement. "You know what you need? A go-around with a beautiful young lady! You can find one on the internet you know. There's one website in particular that's really good," he said, going on to tell me all about it.

"No, I haven't, and I'm afraid to ask how you've heard of it, and you're not talking about a call girl, are you?" I said. asked

"I'm talking about a pleasant distraction, my good friend. They have personal ads on the site where lovely ladies advertise their services." He smiled at me and took another drink.

I couldn't help but let my mind think about it for a moment. "You know, you have the worst ideas ever. I don't understand why they always sound so good," I confirmed.

He got up and smiled. "Have a good night my friend," and he walked to the door and left.

Later that night, as I lay in bed thinking back on the day's experiences, it wasn't Steve's idea that occupied my thoughts, it was the page I had taken a picture of on the computer and the return on investment that intrigued me. By just combining a few ingredients together to form a desirable product and then selling it. What could possibly go wrong?

Chapter 2

Lucy in the Sky

A few weeks went by. I got my licence renewed and moved into the new house. Built in the seventies, it was an older home, but it had character. It had three bedrooms and two bathrooms and was across the street from a small lake, to the north side of the house. The lake provided a nice view from the living room and two of the bedrooms that faced in that way. The lot to the east end of the house was vacant and filled with trees and vines, which gave it a thick, jungle look to it. This was particularly nice, as it provided a good wind barrier from the occasional hurricane that finds the shores of Florida from time to time. Just beyond, a street ran north to south, past the end of the block and a drainage canal, so that there was no connecting road through the east of me. The house to the west was occupied by an older lady; it being Florida, there were many retired people. Her family came to visit on the occasional weekend, but aside from that, she was very quiet. Behind me, I was bordered by a thick brush so that I couldn't see the neighbours. My spare bedroom and kitchen faced in that direction.

What really appealed to me about the neighbourhood, aside from it being much closer to work, was the lack of a homeowners' association. There were no entry gates and no guard shacks. It was a lower middle-class area where people could park their cars in their yards and not fear any repercussions. Unpretentious, yet quiet. Large oak trees flourished throughout, with many being covered in moss. There were several small, natural lakes located all around, which gave the place a peaceful vibe. The lakes were all named, including the one across from me, Lake Laguna. The land bordering the lake was owned by the county and therefore, would not be built on, so I had no neighbours across the street from me. It was not isolating, just airy, which was a nice change from the crowded Palm Beach area which I had just left.

Being closer to work was also refreshing, just twenty minutes from door to door. I became more relaxed and refreshed, not having to drive so much each day. Having more time in my week, I took up fishing, exploring new spots and catching some nice fish. There were snook, redfish and speckled trout, all of which were fun to catch and great to eat. The area reminded me of what my hometown used to be like growing up as a boy; not overcrowded with lots of natural beauty. I knew I had made the right choice to move up here.

One afternoon, while I was exploring one of my new-found fishing holes, I got a text from Tricia.

"How are you? how have you been? It's Tricia by the way."

I couldn't believe it; the text totally caught me off guard. Why was she texting me and for what purpose? My heart raced. Inside my soul, it was like a dark blanket was uplifted and I suddenly became alive.

I texted her back that I still had her programmed in my contacts, so that of course, I knew it was her. She told me about her job and some random events happening in her life, almost as if she were bored and just needed someone to chat with. When I asked her if there were any chance of us getting back together, she told me she was happy in her new relationship, but that we could remain friends, if I liked. Despite feeling like a sucker, I texted her that it would be just fine; I'd rather have her as a friend in my life than not at all. She then texted that she had to get back to work. That was the last I heard of her the rest of the day. But she was all I could think about, and it drove me crazy. She said she was happy in her new relationship, which meant she was seeing someone else now. How could she move on so quickly? I became irritated by the thought.

Later that evening, to get my mind off her and our conversation, I went online and ordered the ingredients needed to make fentanyl. Aside from a couple of hiccups, it was easier than I thought. I used a couple of different chemical companies to avoid attracting suspicion. One gentleman from whom I had to order over the phone, asked me what I was using the compound for. I said I was restoring an old car and needed the chemical to dissolve the rust off the engine parts, given it was a solvent. That seemed to suffice as an explanation, and I was able to complete the order. I found the molecular sieve, which would help bind the chemicals, at Wal-Mart online. So, by spreading the orders over a few companies, I felt confident of avoiding unwanted suspicion. Job well done.

But being a pharmacist by no means qualified me as a chemist, so I ordered a book that explained the chemical process of the Siegfried method, which was used in the home synthesis of fentanyl. There was also the Janssen method, but it was a more complicated way that required equipment only drug manufacturers could afford. The book cost more than the combined cost of the ingredients but was a necessity to produce the drug properly. It would also list the supplies I would need to make it.

The next day after work, I drove to Sam's Club to purchase a metal table that restaurants used in their kitchens to prepare food. I set it up in the spare bedroom facing the backyard to avoid any prying eyes from the street. Other supplies such as goggles and beakers were harder to come by. Due to the past methamphetamine crisis, certain items like those were made less accessible to the public. Fortunately, having a doctorate degree in pharmacy and a national provider identification number, which was given to every medical provider, I was able to eventually find and order everything I needed.

Doing all this was not enough to distract me from thinking of Tricia, which I did while laying alone in my bed at night. It became harder and harder for me to fall asleep and I felt frustrated. So, taking my friend Steve's bad advice, I went on the website he had told me about and searched for local escorts. I couldn't believe the number of women, young and older, who offered their services. Some of these ladies did not look pretty. Why someone would want to see them was baffling to me. It was weird seeing these advertisements and I would have never known about it if not for my friend Steve.

I did come across a picture of an attractive woman I thought looked good. Her advert said she was thirty years old, which was almost twenty years younger than me, but she looked mature. She had a slender build and long, dark hair, but it was her eyes that caught my attention. They were sexy looking, but with a hint of sombre worldliness, as if she was not happy and looking for a change. I took a screenshot of her photo and added her into my contacts. She posted herself as Sky, but I doubted that was her real name.

I texted her number, "Hello Sky."

At first, I got no response, and I felt slightly disappointed, but about five minutes later I got a "Hello sweetie, what can I do for you?"

I became exhilarated at the prospect of meeting her, and I texted that I was interested in a visit. Also, I asked her how much it would cost. She asked if I was affiliated with any law enforcement, to which I said no. Then she quoted me one hundred dollars for a half hour or one hundred and fifty dollars for an hour. I texted that I didn't think I could last an hour, and that a half hour would be just fine, then she asked when. Feeling courageous, I texted back right now, if that was fine with her. She asked for my address, then said she would see me soon.

I suddenly became aware that I had texted my address to someone I had never met before. A slight fear came over me, as I had not done anything like this ever before, but it was twinned with a feeling of exhilaration as well. I pictured myself as Tom Cruise in *Risky Business* after calling Lana, but I was a man, while his character was a teenager. What the hell was I thinking? I showered and got dressed, then waited in the living room, glancing out of the window apprehensively.

After what seemed to be a very long time, I noticed a black Chrysler Pacifica pull up to the front of the house. Sky got out of the front passenger side and started walking up to the front door as the car drove away. I went out to meet her, as she lit a cigarette and smoked by the door.

I introduced myself, "Hello, I'm Paul. You didn't drive yourself?"

She looked calm and relaxed, and replied coolly, "That was my cousin who dropped me. He is going to get some cigarettes at the store and wait for my text to come get me."

For whatever reason, I believed her. She looked like her picture online and was very attractive. I felt a little intimidated by her good looks, but her unpretentious demeanor set me at ease. Her hair was dark and long, well kept, and she had red lipstick on her voluptuous lips. She was very slender but looked healthy. When she was finished smoking her cigarette, I brought her inside. A little nervous, I showed her around the house. I wanted her to feel comfortable and not think there were other people in there, but she did not seem on edge. Feeling a little dorky at that moment, I walked her to my room, where we both sat on the bed.

"Thanks for looking like your picture online," I said to her.

She chuckled and said, "Yeah, I have heard that a lot of girls use old photos of themselves, even on regular dating sites."

"Isn't that the worst," I said, awkwardly.

"Do you have your donation sweetie?" she asked politely.

I took out five twenty-dollar bills and put them on the bed between us. She smiled and put the money in her purse, then we began to undress. I felt self-conscious, as she was very pretty, and younger, but she did not seem to notice. I found myself comparing her body to Tricia's but didn't feel guilty. I just wanted to get over Tricia once and for all. We proceeded to have sex. I had to slow down a few times as I didn't want it to end too quickly. Whatever thoughts I may have had of Tricia melted away, and I was all encompassed in the moment.

Before long, I climaxed and fell onto the mattress exhausted. "That was exactly what I needed, thank you."

"No, thank you," she replied.

She went into the bathroom and got dressed. When she came out, she texted her cousin to come and get her when he was ready, and then we sat on the bed and just started talking about random things.

"How much does it cost to advertise online?" I asked her.

"It costs a few bitcoins to run an ad for a week."

"Oh wow, high tech. The currency of the future," I said.

"Yeah, I'm just doing this to make some extra money," she said, almost as if she were ashamed of what she was doing.

"I hear you," I replied. "I am planning on making a batch of fentanyl and selling it online. The ingredients are cheap, and I can make a lot of money."

I hesitated for a moment, not believing I had just told her that, but for some reason, I felt like being open with her. Perhaps it was my deep-rooted Catholicism and the need to confess my wrong doings to someone, or it just seemed natural to share my secrets with someone I had just had sex with. For whatever reason, I had told her and there was no going back from that.

It set my mind at ease when she said, "Oh that's funny, I used to be the head of a lab that made vitamins."

"Do you want to see something cool?" I asked her.

"Sure," she replied.

I went and got my phone and showed her the screenshot I took of the ingredients needed to make fentanyl, their respective prices, and the retail value once it was made. I even showed her a couple of the items I had received and the room where I had set up the table in.

"Wow, you are serious, aren't you?" she said, sounding impressed.

"Yeah, why not," I replied.

"I'm Lucy by the way, not Sky, in case you want to add me to your contacts."

"I'd like that," I said.

She then went outside and while waiting for the car, lit another cigarette. "Did you enjoy spending time with me?" she asked.

"Yes, very much so," I replied.

"I enjoyed it too," she said. "Will you call me again?"

"Absolutely, but first you have to tell me about your tattoo." I had noticed it while we were making love; it was a rose and stem wrapped with a vine and two hearts on either side of it, one of which was dripping tears.

She looked at me with intense eyes while taking a drag on her cigarette. "The rose is me and the vine represents all the shit that entangles me, all the drama that life tries to choke me with. The hearts represent my mother and father who will always surround me and remind me of our family bond."

"Why does the one heart have tears?" I asked innocently.

"That one represents my father, who passed away last year," she said.

"Oh, I am so sorry," I said, feeling bad for asking.

"Thank you, Paul" she said. The slick black car pulled up to the house and she put out her cigarette. "I hope to hear from you again soon."

Now normally I would have thought she was just trying to sell herself to me, but the fact that she remembered my name and shared that private information about her family with me, I truly believed her. She got into the car and they drove off. It was hard to see who was driving, since it was dark out and the windows were tinted. All I could make out was that the driver was tall. I shook my head with bewilderment, as for some reason, I felt a connection with her. I didn't know why. I went inside and lay down for the night. I fell into a peaceful and guiltless sleep. Perhaps Steve was right, that was exactly what I needed.

Chapter 3

A Revealing Revelation

The next day, I received the main ingredient needed to make my fentanyl, N-phenethyl-piperidone, or NPP for short. It required a signature, and it was the most expensive of the ingredients. I brought the box, labeled hazardous material, inside, placed it on the floor in front of me and sat on the couch. I realised I had no idea what I was doing. I knew I wanted to set up the clandestine lab in my spare back bedroom, and I needed to read the chemistry book I had ordered describing the steps. Unfortunately, the book seemed drab and boring.

I then thought of Lucy, and how she used to manage a vitamin lab, so I texted her to see if she was available one night over the weekend. She replied yes and asked which day and for how long. I texted back suggesting the next day at nine in the evening for an hour, and she replied, "See you then…:)"

I forced myself to read a few chapters of the chemical book, as I affectionately named it. Even though it was dry reading, it turned out to be very informative. I read it off and on with many breaks to keep myself from getting burned out too quickly.

Lucy came over the following night, as discussed. Again, she was dropped off by someone in the same dark car. Something about that model made me think of it being a mobster's car. She came up to the house and had a smoke.

"Is he going to hang around the neighbourhood for an hour?" I asked.

"He's going to the store to wait for my text. Don't worry," she said, as she took a drag.

"He's not really your cousin, is he?"

"No, he isn't," and she leaned forward and gave me a smooch on the cheek. "It's nice to see you again."

I smiled and tried not to blush. We proceeded inside and I noticed she just seemed to be more comfortable, perhaps now being familiar with my place. My eyes followed her body as she walked in. She wore a black tee shirt and blue jean shorts, along with black fishnet stockings that covered her long, seductive legs. She would have easily turned any man's head, and I was definitely distracted by her sexy vibe.

"May I have a soda," she asked.

"Of course, silly, there's some Cokes in the fridge."

She opened the fridge and grabbed a Coke, then headed back to my room. My eyes followed her every move; I was in a trance. We wound up having amazing sex that I wished had lasted longer than it did, but she did not hurry to get dressed afterwards. We lay on the bed, both naked, but covered by my sheets. It felt relaxing and free of burden.

"So, who are you?" I asked, trying not to sound too awkward. I really didn't expect anything deep or meaningful, but her response in earnest, felt genuinely sincere.

"I'm the daughter of a travelling preacher who had immigrated to Miami with my mother from Rio de Janeiro. I remember him riding his bicycle around, preaching to whomever would listen. We didn't have much growing up, but we were never hungry. Then one day, he decided to open a church in the neighbourhood, but he needed money to make that happen. Since he had no steady income, he could not get a bank loan. So, he borrowed some money from a loan shark. Unfortunately, he had a heart attack and became ill, so he never was able to get his church up and running."

She took a sip of her soda, then continued. "Repaying the loan then fell on me, since my mother is an illegal immigrant and barely survives working at a laundromat, so that's how I ended up here, doing this kind of work until his loan is repaid."

Lying there naked together, I took in all she had just told me. It seemed unfair to me that she had to do these things, and her story moved me. I wondered if she was forced into this line of work, and that she was being held against her will, but she had a cell phone and there were no bruises or marks of physical abuse on her. Whatever the case was, I felt for her.

Instead of probing her with questions, I said, "Come with me, I want to show you something."

We got dressed, and then she followed me into the back bedroom. I walked up to the steel table I had set up, turned around to her, and stepped aside so she could see all the items I had gathered to make my first batch of fentanyl. I wanted her to forget why she was there.

Her eyes lit up, "Are these all of the things you needed?" she asked.

"Yes indeed," I exclaimed, smiling.

I mustered a look of utter triumph, feeling accomplished by gathering up such an array of chemicals, beakers, and Bunsen burners. She slowly glided along the table, looking at everything and smiling with a delight that made me gleam inside. I was glad to have distracted her from her sad story.

"It doesn't look like you've made a first batch yet," she observed.

"Well, despite my education and the ability to acquire all these things, I've come to realise I have no idea what I'm doing or how to make it." I giggled after saying that. "Quite embarrassing actually."

"And that's where I come in?" she asked, her eyes shining.

"Well, if you think you're up for the task, sure!" I confirmed.

"I see a couple of things you've missed," she said. "We are making fentanyl, correct?"

"Yes," I replied.

"You realise that pure fentanyl is lethal just by touching it with your bare hands," she stated.

I did not reply but listened to her intently. I was surprised she knew that and that I had overlooked it. She obviously was not as innocent as I had imagined her to be.

"Go and pick up several pairs of rubber gloves, two rubber aprons, a glass tupperware set, and a heat lamp. I will come out for a day to get us started. When is your next day off from work?"

"I am off next weekend from Friday through Sunday," I replied.

"Great, I'll come by Friday at noon. Can you get all of those things by then?"

"I should be able to," I said.

"Are you sure you're ready for this," she asked.

"I think so," I assured her, trying to sound convincing.

She came up to me and planted a big kiss on my cheek. I wanted to tell her that I was glad we had met, but she put her finger up to my lips and shushed me quiet. Her eyes had a look of mischievous delight to them, and I became entranced. She left me standing there and went outside, to smoke a cigarette, I thought, but when I looked out the front window, she was already gone.

Chapter 4

Work, work, work

I was able to find the last few items Lucy asked for on Amazon and have them delivered to the house before Friday. I showed up to my full-time job as usual, never late, yet feeling the drudgery of it. The owner, also a pharmacist, had done very well for himself. He opened his own pharmacy back in 1976, and over the years, was able to purchase the corner block where the pharmacy was situated. In addition to his pharmacy, there was a Mexican restaurant, a cell phone carrier, and a Dunkin Doughnuts in his plaza, so it was a busy location.

Through the years, he also founded a generic drug wholesaler in Tennessee, of which he was now a board member. This allowed him to purchase generic drugs, the majority of which were dispensed in retail pharmacies, at a huge discounted price. This helped boost his profit margins at the pharmacy. Being well established, the place filled, on average, over five hundred prescriptions a day, which was very good for an independent pharmacy. Filling so many scripts every day made for a stressful environment, even with a large staff, but it also made the days pass quickly.

Having been there for almost three years, I knew the staff well, and they knew me. As with any stressful workplace, many technicians came and went, but there were a few that had been there for a long time and liked to work hard, finding it a rewarding place to work. His pharmacy was busier than any of the local competitors, including the nearby Walgreens. He really did build up a nice business and he was proud of what he had achieved. Despite being, what I am sure was a millionaire, he had an air of being a nice person. No one seemed too nervous when he came into work, which wasn't as often as when I had first started working. Now that I was familiar with the intricacies of the workplace, he had more time to devote to the back office and his personnel.

I was thankful to have such a high paying, full time job. After the great recession of 2008, with memories of high unemployment looming in the back of everyone's minds, it was easy to appreciate having a good job. Yet I felt uneasy, wanting something more. No matter how much I made, which usually averaged fifteen hundred dollars a week, it seemed that I was still living paycheck to paycheck. It was my hope that my extracurricular endeavor would provide me that extra breathing space I wanted.

And so, I showed up to work, did my job and said nothing to my co-workers about my plans. I admit that Friday could not have rolled around fast enough, as I was eager to see what Lucy and I could get accomplished. On the morning off, I sat in the living room trying to read the chemistry book, constantly lifting my eyes to see if Lucy had pulled up.

Sure enough, a little before noon, a car came, but it was not the usual black town car she arrived in, but an Uber driver with a red Toyota Corolla. She got out of the back seat and headed up to the house. I went out to greet her while she had a cigarette.

"Hey stranger, how are you?" I asked.

"Good thanks. Say, do you think you can drop me back off at my neighbourhood when we are done later?" she asked, looking a little nervous. "I told them I was going to meet a friend at the mall to go shopping and catch a movie."

"Sure, no problem, don't worry," I said.

"Great, now let's get started," she insisted.

She stomped out her cigarette and we went inside, going directly to the back room. We spent the first couple of hours setting up the Bunsen burners, unpacking the flasks and beakers, and going over the chemical process of synthesizing fentanyl. After grabbing a quick bite to eat in the kitchen; leftover pizza, we headed back in the room, donned our goggles, and began measuring out ingredients. Proceeding as per the instructions in the book, we had to improvise when missing a certain sized flask or beaker.

The process took several hours, but we were both very focused on what we were doing, knowing that the outcome would be rewarding. At one point, it began to rain outside, and the sky darkened. It transported me back to my childhood. I used to love it when it rained while I was at school. For some inexplicable reason, I was able to concentrate clearer and focus better. At other times, I would get distracted easily with conversation, thinking of girls or just plain daydreaming.

Today, with the pouring rain outside, Lucy and I became engrossed in what we were doing. It was our shared objective, being partners, to complete our task. One of us would read from the book, while the other combined ingredients, placed a flask over a flame, put powdery residue onto wax paper; whatever was called for at the time. We were like a silhouette, and by the late afternoon, we had our finished product thinly spread onto a metal tray to dry. It did not look like much, certainly not like say, a kilo of cocaine, but it was worth as much. We waited to weigh it, since it was still moist and then placed it under the heat lamp to dry.

"I don't know about you," I said, "but I'm exhausted. I feel like I've put in a full day's work."

Lucy was looking at the powder intently. "Be sure not to touch this with your bare skin, okay?" she warned me.

"Yeah, of course," I assured her.

"I'd say let's celebrate, but I'm running late. Do you think you can drive me back now?" she asked.

"Sure, no problem," I said.

She looked at the drying powder almost like a mother to a new-born child. We each grabbed a soda from the fridge. She got her purse and then we piled into my car to leave.

"You'll have to tell me where to go," I reminded her.

"I'm in Port Saint Lucie, close to I-95," she told me.

"Oh, okay, that's not too far," I said.

I smiled to set her mind at ease about having to drive her. She looked a little nervous, so I told her she could smoke if she wanted to, but to crack open her window. She did, but I could still tell she was mentally occupied with something. I assumed it was about how we were going to split the proceeds once we sold the batch.

"You know we can split the money half and half once we sell the stuff." I smiled at her again. "Speaking of which, how are we going to sell it?"

"I think online is the safest option," she replied without hesitating. She then asked me if I'd heard of a particular website that she obviously had in mind.

"No, I haven't," I replied. I was surprised there was an online option. I had to think about that as I drove onto the interstate, south towards her town.

"Yeah, it's on the dark web." She said, finishing her cigarette and rolling up her window, as we were going fast now. "You need to download the Tor browser onto your laptop, which scrambles your IP address, then you can open an account on their site."

"I'll have to research that later," I said.

"It's really cool. Everything is purchased and sold with Bitcoin, a digital kind of currency. The Bitcoin can then be converted into cash on various apps like Bitstamp. It's the safest way to sell illegal things online and it's virtually untraceable," she explained.

"It amazes me how much you know about all this," I said, astounded. "So, it sounds like I have some homework to do this week." I winked at her.

"Yeah, it will take you a few days to get that all set up. You won't have to purchase any Bitcoins since all we are doing is selling, but you will need to link your bank account to the Bitstamp app. That is how you can transfer the money."

"Won't that lead back to me somehow?" I asked, concerned.

"No, it won't. The Bitstamp app acts as a buffer between you and the website. Research it and get familiar with it and I'm sure you will get comfortable," she said, leaning over to kiss my cheek.

She directed me to go west on St Lucie West Boulevard, and then to pull into a gas station across the street from a gated development. It was called PGA National and it looked somewhat exclusive. I was impressed.

"Don't you want me to drive you inside?" I asked.

"No, thank you though. I think it's best if you drop me off here." She had that worried look on her face again. "I have another phone number where you can reach me directly if you'd like me to give it to you?" she offered.

"Yes, I'd like that," I said. "I'll programme it under Lucy this time, instead of Sky."

She laughed, then gave me her other number. She reminded me to stir the powder around occasionally until it dried and then turn off the heat lamp. She also warned me not to touch any of it with my bare hands, to always handle it with gloves on. I reassured her that I would be extra careful. Then she gave me a kiss on the lips. She got out of the car and walked across the street, past the gate and then disappeared beyond the wall bordering the community. I realised I could not take my eyes off her whenever she walked away from me.

Chapter 5

From Russia with Love

Lucy walked past the guard who recognised her from his small, yet comfortably air-conditioned guard house. She lit a cigarette as she walked through the upper middle-class neighbourhood. She thought about where she had grown up; the contrast between her hometown and where she was now. There, the people used to wave to each other they passed by, and everyone knew who you were. Even though most people were not rich, they seemed content, unlike here. Despite the large houses with their pristinely manicured yards, palm trees and sheltered fencing, no one ever said hello as you passed by. No greetings were ever exchanged, and if you ever walked near someone, they always avoided facial contact by looking down at their cell phone or just pretended to be busy. Sometimes, she thought that it was her, that she didn't belong here, but honestly, she really didn't care.

The house she lived in was owned by a Russian woman who owned several small businesses in Palm Beach county. It was an investment property, a second home, that for appearances, she would rent out. In fact, it was a house used by the Russian mob to house girls such as herself, for sex trafficking. She lived with five other younger women, and they bunked in pairs. It was a four-bedroom home, and the master room was occupied by Dimitri, a low-level Russian mobster.

Dimitri ran the home by driving the girls to their out calls, providing drugs to them, and handling the money. The syndicate liked to use him for this purpose because he was gay, thereby never taking a personal interest in any of the girls. The girls liked him because he never made advances towards them. Dimitri was in a relationship with a Russian named Igor. The girls disliked Igor very much. He was much bigger than Dimitri, with strong, big limbs and a hairy torso. He also worked for the mob and was much meaner than Dimitri. He was higher up in status and ran the drug trade along the eastern coast of Florida. This kept him busy and he was only able to come visit once a week or so. He also did not want anyone knowing about his personal visits with Dimitri. He always came on the pretense of delivering heroin for the girls of the house, which was true; they all had drug addictions except for Lucy. Once he was there, Dimitri and Igor would go into the bedroom, lock the door, turn up the radio and spend a couple of hours together. Igor would then leave, rather quiet and satisfied looking, without saying anything.

Dimitri on the other hand would tell the girls about his sexual exploits with Igor, which often consisted of black, tight leather outfits, whips and lines of cocaine snorted off each other's chests. This provided the girls with much amusement and created a lot of chatter amongst themselves. Of course, none of this was to be mentioned when Igor or anyone else was around, and since Igor was the one who provided for the girls' habits, they were happy to comply. Igor's need for secrecy was much exacerbated by the fact that he was feared by his fellow constituents and considered a ruthless gang member who reigned with violence and fear, so he did not want anyone knowing about his personal connection with Dimitri, which he considered a weakness. This is why he was sometimes belligerent to the girls, since they would see him spend time there with Dimitri.

Lucy felt sorry for the girls she lived with. They were all younger than her and all had addictions, which is a cruel baggage to carry, and made them do things they would never have considered before; things they now hardly thought twice about doing. Somehow, the Russian mob found them, and they were given a chance to live in a comfortable house, in a comfortable neighbourhood, with a reliable source for their fixes. All that was asked of them in exchange, was to make themselves available for sex, twenty-four hours a day, seven days a week. Between the six of them, it wasn't too taxing, but it was steady, especially on the weekends and holidays.

Lucy was a slightly different case. Her service came about because she owed money to a Russian loan shark. She had no drug dependency, though Dimitri implied that she did, so he had extra for the other girls. He did his best to keep them regulated on an even keel, but addiction has an insatiable appetite at times, so the extra amount came in handy for him.

Lucy saw Igor's car parked in the driveway. She reached the door, took a deep breath, and went in. Igor was standing in the kitchen looking very annoyed, waiting for her to arrive. She noticed all the girls were conspicuously absent, hiding in their rooms.

Walking right up to her, Igor demanded, "Where have you been all day?"

Dimitri was sitting on the couch in the living room.

"I've been out with a friend," she replied.

"Well it has been busy," he retorted in a thick Russian accent, "and the girls had to take on an extra client due to you skipping out. You're going to take on the next six calls that come in!"

"Yeah right," Lucy said sounding disinterested.

Without warning, Igor slapped the side of her face with the back of his right hand. The blow caused her to fall to the floor. She was startled and angry, but instinctively she knew he wanted her to cry, so she did. Dimitri remained seated on the couch, though he could see everything that happened. She pulled herself up slowly and leaned on the marble countertop.

"I'm sorry," she said, "I don't know what came over me."

He looked at her coldly, then said, "Dimitri will make sure you get your work in tonight."

He picked up his keys that were on the counter and left, slamming the door shut behind him. Once he was gone, the other girls came out to help her. Her roommate fetched a small bag of ice and wrapped it with a washcloth while the others walked with her to the couch where Dimitri sat. They all counseled her nicely while she gently held the ice next to her cheek. The pain was piercing, and she knew it would bruise. Lucy knew it was a scare tactic that Igor used to inflict order amongst them, and that Dimitri would not interfere on her behalf. She also had a plan that required her to remain complacent for the moment and not retaliate. It was nice of the others to come out and comfort her.

The youngest one said, "I've got the next call," and stroked Lucy's hair.

Dimitri did not balk at this, and he let them be while they all fussed around Lucy.

"Thank you, Hailey," Lucy said to her, "but you really don't have to do that for me."

Being the youngest one of the girls there, the others had taken on a protective vibe towards Hailey, and they all cared about her very much, especially Lucy. It felt strange that now Hailey was taking on a protective role, and Lucy felt ashamed. She felt a little guilty as well. Hailey had just turned eighteen, and she was basically kicked out of her home due to her drug addiction. She was very petite and innocent looking, but her habit was no less than any of the other girls.

"It's okay," Hailey told her. "We girls have to stick together."

Lucy hugged her, then went into the bathroom to take a long, hot bath to relax. She hated this place, the culture and all the people that lived here. It was not home to her, and visions of vindication bubbled up from within. The heat from her bath water steamed up the mirror. She thought of her day with Paul and how they worked so well together. Taking out her private phone that she hid from Dimitri, she texted Paul, "thinking of you ☺"

Chapter 6

A Beautiful Day in the Neighbourhood

I did as Lucy had instructed, researching Bitcoin and its uses for online sales. I opened a Bitstamp account and linked my bank account to it. I also opened a seller's account on the website she had mentioned. I had to download a Tor browser, and a programme called Onion, which basically shielded my IP address while using the site and made all transactions anonymous. I browsed the site and was amazed at what you could purchase there online: all prescription drugs, illicit drugs and even firearms. The site gave sellers ratings based on feedback given by buyers. There were people selling Xanax, Vicodin, and Percocet by the tablet and in bulk. There were not as many people selling illicit street drugs such as cocaine and heroin, and fewer still that I could find, selling fentanyl. I was not sure if that was a good thing for us or not.

I also delved into the dark web, where the website we were going to use operated. It turned out that the dark web was hundreds of times larger than the regular web that most people used. I saw an analogy describing it as the mass of ice below water that no one sees, compared to the regular web as just the tip of the iceberg. It had a much larger content of information than the commonly used web which was geared mostly towards consumerism. You could find any book ever written on the dark web plus information some might call privileged. This included government documents, architecture plans and even steps on how to synthesize drugs, legal and illicit. There was no search engine like Google to help guide you, but there were sites that helped explain how to manoeuvre through it. I suddenly became aware of a whole subculture of people who shared information through chat rooms and disguised social networking sites.

I did not spend all my time pursuing methods of bending the law. I also took up jogging, mostly in the mornings. I think it helped me feel like a normal adult. I would usually only jog a mile or so, not very far, as I'd never liked it. When I would arrive back at my block, I would walk the rest of the way to cool down. This allowed me to observe my neighbours.

About six lots down, on the other side of the street, there was a sheriff's deputy that worked in the crime scene division. He parked the work van out front of his house on the yard. Across from him on my side of the street was a two-story house, which was not common in the neighbourhood. They owned a business called Natural Weed Killer. From what I could tell, all their sales were done online, as they never seemed to leave their home, and every afternoon they had a stack of boxes that were picked up by FedEx. On the side of the Toyota Tacoma they owned was their website address, in all green but no company phone number, just the website. It was the first time I noticed someone running a business from their home.

I did have to chuckle to myself as one afternoon, driving home from work, I saw a semi-truck parked in front of their house with the name of a chemical company on it. The driver was offloading a couple of barrels and hauling them up to the house. In fact, I noticed that they must have packaged their product inside the garage, as I could see stacks of boxes inside, as well as numerous green spray bottles.

"So much for the 'All Natural,'" I thought to myself.

One morning, while walking down the block after a jog, I met one of my neighbours and his small dog. He was taller than me and balding. If I had to guess, I would say he was in his late fifties. He was not unfit, but he also looked as if he disliked the gym. His dog was adorable. She looked like a miniature border collie with black and white fur.

"Welcome to the neighbourhood," he said.

Obviously, he could tell I was new, which made him observant. He did not come off as being nosy, which was settling to me. He lived just a few houses away from me on the opposite side of the street and next door to the gentleman who worked for the crime scene division.

"Where are you from," he asked nicely.

"I'm a Florida native. I grew up in Jupiter," I replied.

"Ah, a Florida native," he said inquisitively. "Those are rare to come by these days."

"I'm Paul." I put out my arm and we shook hands.

"Nice to meet you. I'm George and this little cutie is Cassie." He smiled down at her. "I used to work on Jupiter Island you know. I helped lay all the fiber optic lines on the north end of the island there."

"Oh, very prestigious area," I said, recalling that some of the wealthiest people lived on the north end, including the Ely Lilly family.

He smiled, "Yes, all of the millionaires out there have high speed internet thanks to my company." He seemed proud of the fact. "What brings you to the Vero Beach area?"

"Work," I replied.

"Oh, what do you do?"

"I'm a retail pharmacist for an independent pharmacy."

"Interesting, well if you ever need help with your internet connection, let me know." He called for Cassie who had wandered off to take care of her business, and then shook my hand goodbye.

I eyed the house across the street from his and saw video cameras installed in several places on the house. I thought it a little odd, as the person who lived there had a pool cleaning truck and a homemade wood trailer attached carrying his supplies. I brushed it off as paranoia, but I did think it might be worth investing in some cameras for my house, especially given my new-found interest in chemicals.

I got a text from Lucy saying she was coming over this Saturday and that she was looking forward to seeing me. I had carefully stored the fentanyl powder in a glass container and took several pictures of it with my phone ready to upload onto the dark web. I wanted to wait until Lucy arrived to list it but transferred the pictures over to my laptop computer. This suddenly made me nervous since I was pretty sure the photos were being stored on my I-Cloud account, even if I were to delete them from my files. I figured that might be a good question to ask George the neighbour, since he seemed a little techy.

The next day, Friday, while I was home, I kept a random eye out for him. Around noon, I saw him walking Cassie toward the lake, so I tried to look as if I had just randomly walked outside, then wandered over to see him. He looked happy to see me.

"Hey neighbour," I said, "how is Cassie doing?"

"Oh, she is getting old these days. She doesn't like to walk as far as she used to. How are you?" he asked.

"Doing well thanks. Hey, I had a silly question I was thinking about and thought you might know the answer."

He looked intrigued. "Okay, fire away."

"Well I was wondering if the I-Cloud stores photos you take on the phone or laptop, even if you delete them from your devices?"

He pondered this for a moment. "Not for long. The photos are kept on there for thirty days after you delete them, then erased. Apple has a solid reputation for privacy. They were once subpoenaed by the government to unlock the I-phone of a suspected terrorist and they refused, citing privacy issues."

"Well that certainly is reassuring," I said, delighted. Then out of curiosity, I asked, "Do you know how to design websites?"

"Yes, I can write code to develop a site. I don't do it much now that I am retired, but I would be glad to help if you had something in mind." He seemed happy to offer the assistance.

"Thank you," I said. "I just may get back to you on that. Enjoy your day; it's a beautiful one out."

"Yes, it is, thanks," he replied, as we parted ways.

It had occurred to me that selling drugs directly from our own website would be more prosperous since we would not have to pay a seller's fee. But I wasn't really sure if the demand would warrant all the extra work involved. I decided to see how long it would take to sell the fentanyl on the site we had chosen and go from there. If it sat on the site for days on end, we might have to break it down into smaller quantities. That would mean we would incur more charges. My hopes were not set very high, but still I couldn't help feeling exhilarated by accomplishing something new, and yes, illegal. Even though, it was not as if I had gone out and robbed a bank or stolen a car. It was a victimless crime, and all done from the comfort of my own home. That night, I could hardly sleep, as I lay in bed contemplating all the possibilities that awaited me.

Chapter 7

Fade to Black and Blue

The next day, Lucy arrived via an Uber driver again. I let her in and immediately saw her cheek had been bruised by what looked like a hit to the face. It had begun to pale somewhat, and I could tell she had put some makeup on it to try and cover it up.

"Hey, what happened?" I asked, concerned.

She hesitated a little, placed her purse on the kitchen table, then grabbed a bottled water from the fridge and sitting down on the couch, she said, "Oh, don't worry, it was a silly argument that got a little over heated."

She looked at my entertainment centre, which was crammed full of DVD's, then walked up to it and looked at some of them. "You have a lot of good movies. We should have a movie night and make some popcorn."

My attention swayed from her bruised face to her blue jean shorts. They were very short, revealing her soft, sexy legs. The bottoms of her shorts were frayed, and her black shoes with white socks underneath seemed to compliment her body.

"I'd like that. Any night you want, I'm always here. You're welcome over anytime."

She smiled and gave me a kiss on the cheek. "Thank you, I appreciate that. So how is the powder doing?"

We both smiled, and I led her to the back bedroom. "Have a look," I suggested.

She squatted down even with the metal table and eyed it. "Did you list it yet?"

"No, I wanted to wait for you. Do you want to sell it in one bulk amount? I weighed it this week and it's almost twenty grams. That's almost twenty thousand dollars-worth of product. I'm not sure if anyone will have that kind of money to purchase it all at once." I tried not to sound doubtful, only sincere.

"Why not give it a try anyway," she said confidently. "So, let's list it."

"I already have photos on my computer," I informed her.

"Great," she said. "Did you get started on that site I told you about?"

"All set!" I smiled with pride, like when a child is asked by their mother if they had finished all their homework and they had.

We listed it for an even sixteen thousand dollars. We saw a couple of accounts selling it for a gram at a time, and our price was much better. We figured we would discount it, since we were selling it in bulk. We also put in the item description that it was highly pure and needed to be handled with caution as direct contact could be lethal. I was a little hesitant to say that, as I thought it would scare buyers away, but on the contrary, Lucy thought the opposite.

"Our buyers want as pure and strong a product as they can get their hands on," she explained.

And so, we put it on the active sale screen, then decided to go out into the living room to watch a movie together. Lucy scanned over my DVDs and picked out *Blow*. She seemed enthused by the case, looking at it.

"I've heard many things about this George Jung," she told me.

"You've never seen this movie?" I asked.

"No, I haven't," she replied.

"Oh, I'm sure you will enjoy it," I assured her.

So, I put the movie into my Xbox to play and then went to the bedroom to get us a blanket. I came out and we snuggled together, watching the movie. Even though I had seen it before, it was fun watching it with someone who had not. Her reactions were stimulating to say the least, and a couple of times, she yelled at the characters in Spanish. It was fun.

"How cool is this," I thought to myself.

I felt comfortable having her over, and it was nice to have female company. We seemed to relax together without feeling awkward. It was like discovering someone new and learning all their quirks, but by having jumped into it backwards, since we had already been intimate together.

After the movie was over, she wanted to see if we had sold the fentanyl yet. I hardly expected it to have moved, but she seemed excited to look. So, we signed into the website, and to my amazement, it had sold for the full asking price. Our account was already credited in Bitcoin, minus the website's selling fee. The buyer's shipping address was in our inbox. There were no special instructions, and I noticed it was going to an address in Miami.

"Holy shit," I exclaimed, "do you want to make more?"

Lucy looked extremely happy. Without saying anything, she gently took hold of my hands and led me to the bedroom. She slowly unbuttoned my shirt, looking at me seductively. Then she undid my jeans and I quickly kicked them out of the way, anxious for what was in store. She purposely undressed herself slowly, building up the anticipation. First her shirt, then her bra. I wanted to caress her breasts, but she put out her pointer finger and waved no. I was all worked up, and she pulled me onto the bed, pleasing me with her mouth. It was very erotic.

We made love for quite a while, unrushed and passionately. It felt amazing and I was quite satisfied.

Afterward, we lay together in bed and began to talk, much like we had done the first time, but even more in a relaxed state.

"So, what are you going to do with your money?" I asked.

"I am going to save it until I have enough to pay off what I owe," she said.

She smiled and I could tell she began to see some light at the end of whatever long, dark tunnel she was in. I was going to ask her how much she still owed, but figured it was really none of my business. Instead, I offered her a safe haven.

"You know you are welcome to stay here if you'd like. I have a couple of spare bedrooms as you know."

"That's very sweet of you, but I don't want to take advantage," she said politely.

"You're not. You wouldn't be." I didn't want to press her, but I was concerned for her safety. "I'm just worried about you, given what you have told me, and the fact that you have a bruised face." I felt bad for mentioning it again.

She lay there pondering for a few moments. "I just don't want to get you involved in something you shouldn't be."

"Hey, I'm a big boy, I can handle myself," I told her confidently.

"I know you're a big boy," she smiled wryly.

I rolled over to her and started tickling her along her rib cage. She started to giggle but was able to roll me off quickly. She straddled on top of me and pinned me down on the mattress. I was surprised by how strong she was, given her petite build.

"You're a big boy, are you," she asked, grinning.

"Well, I didn't want to hurt you, so I didn't resist."

"Ah ha," she replied, smiling, as we both knew I was lying.

We both got dressed and decided to get online and order the five ingredients needed to make our next batch. This time, I ordered triple the amounts, feeling confident we could sell our product quickly. Lucy watched, as I ordered, much easier this time, seeing as I was a repeat customer. I did not have to explain to anyone why I was ordering the chemicals given I was already in their system as a client.

"Hey, do you think we can go to Wal-Mart and pick up a couple of things," she asked me.

"Aw darling, how domestic of you," I mocked. "I actually need to get some groceries anyway, so let's go."

I drove us to Wal-Mart, and I grabbed some food items. Aside from a small bag of chips to munch on, the only things she chose were a bottle of cement glue and a can of ground coffee. I thought that intriguing.

"Are you going to do an art project?" I asked sarcastically.

"You'll see," she said.

That made me a little nervous as I didn't know what to expect from her at times. When we got back, she donned a pair of gloves, opened the coffee can, and poured about half of the grounds into a glass beaker. She then put the fentanyl inside a zip lock sandwich bag and placed it inside the can. She put the coffee grounds from the beaker back inside the can and then carefully sealed it back up using the cement glue. Glancing at it, you couldn't tell that the seal had been opened. She wiped the coffee can clean of any fingerprints and then found an empty box to put it inside.

"That was a clever idea," I said admiringly.

"Now you can ship it out on Monday, just be sure to use a 'dummy' return address on it."

"Got ya," I replied. "But what is the best way to ship it?" I was a bit nervous going into a government run post office to mail off illegal drugs.

"I would take it to one of those 'Pack and Ship' stores and have it mailed via Fed-Ex." She seemed rather confident.

"Won't Fed-Ex have drug sniffing dogs at their warehouses?" I asked concerned.

"No silly, that is only for international packages, mostly inbound, not for domestic packages."

"Oh, okay," I said. I felt like asking her how she knew that, but deep down, I really didn't want to know.

"Just be sure to use cash when paying them," she emphasised.

"Good point," I said and smiled.

We then transferred our Bitcoin proceeds to my Bitstamp account. She wanted her half of the money in cash, so I transferred it into my bank account. I asked her if she wanted to add her bank account onto the Bitstamp app, but she declined.

"This way I have a good reason to come see you again soon," she said.

I transferred the other half into my online stocks and shares account. That way I was able to keep the amount of cash I transferred just below ten thousand dollars. She seemed impressed that I had such an account and that I picked my own stocks without the help of a broker. I wished it was at a much higher value than where it was now.

It was starting to turn into the late evening, so she had me drive her back to the same place as I had done the week before. She told me to ask for her tomorrow under her Sky contact if I wanted to have her over again. My eyes followed her as she walked away from the car, noticing her sexy legs and her seductive walk. For some reason I just could not keep my eyes off her, entranced by her physique. Later that night, she called me, and we chatted for over an hour. It was just small talk and how much we enjoyed each other's company. We felt untouchable, or so I thought.

Chapter 8

Mad Money

Lucy and I saw each other regularly in the coming weeks. I would often pay an additional fee to have her spend the night, and in the morning the same black car would come to pick her up. That was fine when I worked at the pharmacy during the week, but on the weekends, I wanted to see her more. I began to long to be with her all the time, almost like an addiction.

As we got more comfortable with each other, she told me about Dimitri, the man in charge of the house she stayed at and drove her around. She also told me about Igor, his male lover, and their strange practices together. I was amused by this somewhat but concerned for her safety as well. Whenever I suggested she leave, she insisted it wasn't that easy. It was as if they held an invisible string to her that kept her attached.

She told me about the girls that lived there with her, and how they watched over each other. She had taken a bit of a motherly role with the youngest one, Hailey, who she seemed to care about very much. I concluded that Lucy and these girls were a steady source of income for them and that no amount of money offered to them would pay off any debt they were owed.

Our income grew proportionately with our increased batch sizes. I was careful to always keep my checking account below ten thousand dollars for fear of attracting the attention of the IRS, who I feared more than the police. It seems that after the explosion of wealth in the eighties by the criminal element, all fueled by cocaine and crooked bankers, the banking industry was mandated to contract outside companies to watch for suspicious activity, to be watch dogs of a sort. The main purpose of these companies was to prevent money laundering in the United States banking system. Researching this on the dark web, I found out that these companies implemented algorithms into spy software that could detect suspicious movements of money. This all made me very nervous, to say the least.

Lucy thought I was being paranoid. It wasn't as if we were pulling in millions of dollars every week, and I understood her point, but I remained cautious just the same. She kept her money in cash, which we put in a large rubber tote bag stored in my spare bedroom. She never seemed worried about how much was in there or the fact that I had access to it at any time. She just felt it prudent to keep it with me than to take it with her to the house where she was staying. I put the collection of personal photographs my mother had given me before she passed away, on top of her cash, that way disguising that there was a pile of money underneath it, just in case someone's prying eyes might stumble upon it.

She liked that I invested my cash into the stock market, and we would often sit together to watch Mad Money on television to learn more about it. Certain stocks would stand out to me for some reason, and I began to follow their prices daily. One in particular, was owned and operated by a billionaire. There was no question the man was an engineering genius, but for the life of me, I could not figure out why his stock was trading around two hundred dollars a share. The company had never posted a profit. On the contrary, it consistently reported losses quarter after quarter. I then noticed one evening, while scanning over its chart, that the price swung above and below two hundred dollars over fifteen times in the last year alone. It occurred to me that if someone were to purchase put and call options on the stock price, it would be very easy to make money. The billionaire himself was fined twenty million dollars by the SEC for tweeting he had secured a private equity firm to buy the company that would value the stock at over three hundred dollars a share. Upon him doing so, the price immediately shot up much higher, but then, when it was revealed that in fact that was not the case, the stock price receded.

I saw all of this as a good opportunity. Whenever the price rose above two hundred, I bought put options to sell, and when it dropped back below two hundred dollars, I bought call options. I made a tidy profit by doing this, and impressed Lucy all the more. It seems the stock market is based more on speculation than actual fundamentals.

I eventually convinced Lucy to open her own Bitstamp account. We found it easier to move Bitcoin around and even noticed its value rise quickly over the short time we had been using it. In fact, I started keeping my money in Bitcoin alone versus risking it on the stock market.

But unfortunately, over time, as with anything that is repeated over and over, our endeavor became more like work, no matter how much income it produced for us. Between ordering the chemicals and supplies, making the fentanyl, listing, and shipping it, cleaning the beakers with special detergents, and then figuring out what to do with the profits, it became like a full-time job. I felt like I was running around like a headless chicken, with no time to just enjoy myself.

As it turned out, one afternoon while chatting with George, I found out that the gentleman across the street from him, who owned the pool cleaning business, was a retired private investigator. Now, I always equated these people as being a bit seedy, and I wondered if perhaps, he was. I asked for an introduction, and George was happy to do so. We walked over and knocked on the door, and the man came to answer.

"Dan, this is Paul, our new neighbour just up the road."

Dan came out and shook my hand. He was older than both of us, and he had a subtle look about him that told a story of one who had seen many troubling things in his lifetime. He was well sunned and in good shape for his age. George left us to get acquainted. We hit it off immediately. While talking, I found out that he had been discharged by the Polk County Sheriff's office many years ago, so he became a private detective. He told me he had one client he worked for who was very wealthy and liked to bend the rules. As a result, this kept him busy cleaning up after him. He left it at that, but I could tell Dan worked for a crooked man.

I was surprised that he was willing to divulge so much about himself, especially having just met, but then I realised that he didn't care what anyone thought of him. He was getting on in age and lived his life with no regrets. This made him a direct person who wasn't afraid to tell someone how things were.

"What happened to the man?" I asked him directly.

"He was murdered," he replied. He didn't expand further. "I enjoy the simple life now, being a pool man. I get lots of sun, being outdoors, and it is relaxing."

I looked up at the small video cameras placed strategically around his house. He went on as if to draw my attention away from them. I didn't ask him about them.

"I often jump into people's pools to cool off and swim around, especially in the summer months when a lot of people flock to their second homes up north. This cost me a few clients though who would find out by reviewing their video cams they had placed outside their homes." He chuckled at the thought of this and did not seem too concerned about losing clients this way. I was impressed with his candor.

"Would you be interested in picking up some extra work?" I asked innocently enough.

"Sure, why not?"

I think he could tell I was not in need of a pool person. He seemed wise beyond his years about criminal activity. He eyed me, not suspiciously, but as if he were sizing me up.

"Great, let me run it by my partner first and I will get back to you," I said.

"You can get hold of me at this number anytime, day or night," he said showing me the number on his phone, and I programmed it under his name in my cell.

I went back to the house and pondered this for a day, then the next evening, ran the idea by Lucy. "I've been thinking it might be a good idea to add a third person onto our venture; a paid employee of sorts."

She looked at me cockeyed.

"There is always something that needs to be done, and between my job and you gone all day, plus everything involved with our venture, I just don't have any free time." I tried not to sound frustrated, just truthful.

"Would it help if I moved in here," she asked.

"Well, I didn't think that was an option," I replied.

"What if it was, would you like that?" she asked me expectantly.

"Why yes, of course I would," I confirmed. I felt relieved a bit that she had offered. "But what about Dimitri? Wouldn't he come looking for you?" The last thing I wanted was to have her 'minders' knocking on my front door in search of their property, so to speak.

She contemplated the question for a minute. "If I don't say anything to the other girls or Dimitri; just had you pick me up one afternoon at the gas station, we should be alright," she suggested.

"How about tomorrow?" I asked.

I was anxious to get her away from that place. It was a Saturday, and I had paid for her to spend the entire evening here with me. She sat down and gave it some more thought.

"Perhaps we should cut this day short, make it look like we had an argument or something. I will call Dimitri to come get me; he won't make me take another call since I'm all paid up for the evening. Just be at the gas station tomorrow at noon to get me," she said.

I thought it was an excellent plan. She called Dimitri, faking as if there had been an argument between us, and asked him to come get her. She looked a little apprehensive.

"Thank you, babe," I said.

She smiled but her eyes looked worried. We sat on the couch together waiting for Dimitri to show up. She turned on the Cartoon Channel and we watched *The Ren & Stimpy Show*. It seemed to help her anxiety, and I was thoroughly amused by it. Finally, the familiar black car showed up, and I finally got a glimpse of Dimitri as he got out of the car. He was tall and muscular, with short blonde hair. She gave me a quick peck on the lips, then went out to the car and got in. I thought perhaps Dimitri might come up to the house to say something threatening to me, but he stayed by the car. He didn't have to. I could tell by looking at him through my living room window that he was a man that could easily kill someone without breaking a sweat.

That night, excited to have her move in, I could hardly sleep. We were taking our friendship to the next level. Friendship. What else could I call it? I couldn't call it a relationship given the inauspicious way we met, but we seemed to have evolved into something.

The next day, I got to the gas station early. As I waited in the car for her, I noticed several company vehicles parked and workers going inside. It said there was a barbeque diner inside, so I wandered inside to have a look. Besides the gas station portion of the store, there was a luncheon diner with several countertop tables inside. These were filled with lawn maintenance workers, construction crew workers and even a few police officers. They were all eating barbeque pulled brisket sandwiches, and it smelled amazing inside. I knew I had stumbled onto a gem. I walked up and ordered a lunch special. A young lady wrote down my order on a ticket and then gave me a slip to pay for it back at the front of the store. I grabbed a bottled soda and paid for my meal, then waited. The young lady looked at me and waved me over. She checked to make sure I had paid, then gave me my sandwich. Since it was crowded inside, I went out and sat at a picnic table that was on the side of the building under a large tree.

I devoured the sandwich which was absolutely delicious. I then understood why so many working-class people came here for their lunch. It was great food at an affordable price. I got a text from Lucy that she was on her way. It was a good place to pick her up, what with all the people coming and going. Between people buying gas or going in to eat, I felt unnoticed by everyone.

I finally saw her approaching. She had a pink duffle bag over her shoulder and her purse in her hand. It was hot out and she wore her jean shorts. She looked good.

"Hey sexy," I yelled out to her, "you going my way?"
She shook her head, "You're such a dork."

She got into the car and we drove off together, happy, and exhilarated. It was perfect.

Chapter 9

Mama Mia

Lucy looked happy and relieved when she got in the car. She also was more peppy than usual. I was glad to see her in good spirits. I can only imagine what it was like living under the constraints and demands of the Russian mob.

"So, I made an appointment with an immigration lawyer down in Miami for this coming Friday," she smiled. "I was wondering if you'd like to come? You can get to meet my mother."

I was surprised she wanted me to do so. She had been talking about getting her mother's immigration status legalised for some time now. She also wanted to get her a nice condo near Miami Beach and away from the laundromat she worked at. It was very noble of her and I admired her for wanting to help her mother out.

"Of course I want to go," I told her.

That week, we got a big shipment of ingredients in, which she was able to bring in the house while I was at work. It was nice having her there in the house with me. I was not sure if she would sleep in my bed or in the spare room, and I did not want to pressure her to do anything she wasn't comfortable with. But she unpacked her stuff, what little there was, into one of my dresser drawers, and she also slept in the bed with me.

It was a big move for me, as I had not lived with another woman since my breakup with Trish. It was a welcome change. I was slightly afraid that the difference in our age might get in the way of our relationship, not that it mattered to me. She was seventeen years younger than me after all, but I was amazed at our conversations, and how at ease she seemed to be with me. Even though there was a generation gap between us, we clicked very well together. She even enjoyed the same movies as I did.

One night, as we were lying down to go to sleep, she asked, "Have you ever made out to Marc Anthony's *Tu Amor Me Hace Bien*?"

"No, I haven't" I said. "In my last relationship I had to endure listening to depressing *Adele* songs while in bed."

"Oh, that sucks," she said with a sarcastic voice.

She pulled up the song on YouTube on her phone and played it. She started getting into the beat, moving her head to the rhythm. She got undressed and I quickly followed suit.

"Feel the music in your body," she commanded me.

I was entranced by her body, which was now swaying in unison with the song. She let down her hair and straddled herself on top of me. Her hair moved freely around, and she sang along to the song. I watched, mesmerised by her beauty and the warmth of her body. We began to make out, her on top of me, both of us moving to the beat of the song. It was the most intimate encounter I had ever had, and I felt like we had shared something special together.

After we climaxed, we lay there together, listening to other Mexican love songs. It was nice to experience it, a welcome change. It certainly helped me to forget my recent break up.

"I feel like I am really beginning to know you," I told her after.

"Ha," she exclaimed. "You don't know me completely, maybe forty percent."

Feeling love struck, I said, "Well, I'll take it."

We both laughed and eventually, fell asleep in each other's arms. It was the best I had felt in a long time. I was beginning to feel something inside of me that I thought I could not gain back.

That Friday, we drove down to Miami together. I had been down that way last year to see the men's final at the ATP Miami Open Tennis Championships. I was privileged to see Roger Federer beat his opponent that year but remembered the long drive to get there. The traffic was just as bad as I had remembered it, though we were not in the same area. Some stretches of the interstate down there were gridlocked. She enjoyed pointing out the huge green iguanas that sunned themselves on the white rocks bordering the canals that ran alongside I-95. These lizards were quickly becoming an invasive species in south Florida, but they were really cool to look at.

We finally got to her mother's apartment complex after nearly two hours. It was not upscale, and the buildings were painted a pale pink. The area looked unkempt and it reeked of poverty.

Since we were running behind schedule, she ran up to her mother's door to get her. I waited in the car with the engine running. I gathered that most of the people who lived there were of Hispanic descent. There were women who had small carpets hanging over the rails of the upstairs apartments and were hitting them with brooms to clean them. There were also small children playing near the dumpster at the end of the complex. There were many stray cats scampering by as well. The sight made me appreciate the house I lived in.

Lucy's mother came out and they hugged. They looked happy to see each other, almost as if they hadn't been together for a long time. Her mother was short in stature and about sixty years old. They were chatting together as they came up to the car. I got out of the car to greet her. I could tell she was a kind person by looking at her, and she smiled at me as they approached.

"Hello," I said, as they walked up and put my hand out to shake hers.

"Oh, she doesn't speak any English," Lucy informed me, but her mother smiled and shook my hand anyway.

I had picked up some of the language while attending college and wanted to try to impress her. There was a heavy Hispanic presence in Broward County, where I went to a private college, especially in the neighbourhood I lived in at the time. It was a small fifty-five and over community across from the college. A nice older couple let me rent a spare room from them. They were quiet, which was fine with me as I was often studying, and they were glad to have the extra rental income. In the house behind them I had met a single Hispanic lady who lived alone. She must have been at least fifty-five, having a home there, but she looked much younger. She loved to cook, and knowing I was a student, would often make me wonderful Hispanic dishes. But there was a catch, in that she would only give them to me when I spoke Spanish. Seeing that I enjoyed her cooking so much, I quickly learned to speak broken Spanish.

I gave it my best and said, "Nice to meet you," in Spanish, but I am sure she could tell I was struggling.

I was not sure how much Lucy had told her about us, so I kept things on a platonic level between us. Her mother smiled and was polite, and we all got into the car to leave for the appointment. They were excited to see each other, and they talked back and forth enthusiastically. I concentrated on driving, but Lucy would give me a recap of what they were discussing so as not to make me feel left out, or so I thought.

We made it to the lawyer's office, which was in a strip mall plaza off Highway 441. It was a dingy looking building, but the office was very busy with a secretary answering calls and collecting paperwork from other clients. The office specialised in immigration law. The lawyer came out and was eager to see them, apparently expecting them. He was tall and slender but had a thick head of dark hair. He wore a cheap looking suit but carried himself with a confident air that gave the impression he was capable at his job.

They went inside his office and I waited out in the lobby. I sat and thumbed through some magazines, observing the coming and going of the people who either worked there or were clients. About twenty minutes later, they emerged, shaking hands, and looking happy about whatever had transpired. Speaking only in Spanish, he seemed to assure them.

Looking content, Lucy said, "He is going to get her legal status to live here in the United States."

"Oh, that's great," I said happily. Her mother smiled and shook my hand.

"She is very happy. Do you mind if we grab a bite to eat on the way back?" Lucy asked.

"Of course not," I replied smiling.

We stopped at a quaint Mexican restaurant to eat, before dropping her mother back to her apartment. They were very exuberant. I thought we could have picked a fancier place to eat, but her mother seemed most appreciative of the gesture. The food was actually very good, and I ate a hearty meal. We dropped her off after eating, and she said goodbye to me while shaking my hands and smiling. She was a very nice lady, I could tell.

*

Dimitri welcomed Igor in, patting him on the back as they headed into the room. Igor reached into a black leather bag and gave him the weekly allotment of heroin along with two boxes of insulin syringes for the girls. Dimitri opened the safe that was in the closet and put the supplies inside, then removed the ledger and cash from the week's income. He kept track of each girl's contribution, as he liked to call it. Igor put the cash in his bag, as was customary, and then he scanned through the ledger book.

"Why the hell isn't Lucy's name in here all week, has she been sick?" he asked.

"No, she's gone on an unauthorised sabbatical," Dimitri replied.

"What the fuck does that mean," Igor asked, annoyed. "Did she get your permission?"

"No, she just up and left the other day and didn't return," Dimitri confirmed.

Dimitri had a good idea where she was, given she had only seen the one client for the past several weeks now. He had driven her there on most of the occasions and found it curious that the man wanted to spend so much time with her. He had heard the girls gossiping that perhaps Lucy was beginning to fall for this guy, given how much time they spent together. A gentler side of him was happy for her, finding someone steady to see on a regular basis, but he knew it would eventually lead to problems, as she was the syndicate's property.

"Does she need me to break out my metal snip cutters to teach her a lesson?" Igor asked, irritated.

Dimitri could tell he was getting agitated. "She knows what is at stake."

Igor scoffed, "Perhaps we need to remind her of that. I can drive down to Miami and snuff out her mother tonight!"

Immediately Dimitri replied, "No, let me handle this. I will get her tomorrow morning, for now let me take care of you."

He got out a bottle of baby oil from his dresser drawer and then opened the other side of his closet. He began to undress while picking out a couple of whips from the array of leather items that hung from the rack inside. Then he went over and played a CD of Russian rock music, blaring it loudly so that the girls would not be able to hear them. They began to kiss, then Dimitri started lashing Igor's back with it.

Igor had risen up the ranks of the Russian mob quickly. He was looked upon with fear and respect, but here, with Dimitri, it felt good to let someone else take control. He felt at ease with Dimitri and had grown close to him. It was with Dimitri he could share his fears and deepest secrets, without judgment. He was able to relax and be himself.

They concluded their sex after an hour or so. Igor took a shower and got dressed. He soon left without bringing up the subject of Lucy again. He knew that Dimitri would take care of it.

*

The next day, I woke up before Lucy did. It looked like a beautiful morning. We were now in the gloomy winter season, but today the sky was clear and blue. There was not a cloud to be seen. The temperature had dropped almost thirty degrees over the last few days, and the cold wind brought with it dark and ominous clouds; but this morning it was crisp and sunny.

I began to warm up the Keurig for my morning cup of coffee when I heard a car door close outside. I peeked around the corner and out the living room window to see a tall, lean man approaching the front door. He was well dressed, in a black sweater, and black trousers. He moved swiftly and with ease, and he looked like he was in good shape as far as I could tell. Squinting to get a better look, I saw that it was Dimitri.

Then I recognised the car. It was the same black Chrysler that used to drop Lucy off before she moved in here with me. My body suddenly went into a flight or fight state and I could feel a sense of anxiety run through me.

I opened the door before he could knock, and I motioned for him to come in. He gave me a look that seemed to say he appreciated it and that we both knew why he was here. He came inside.

Looking me straight in the eyes, he said, "I'm here for Sky."

Wanting to put some space between him and myself, I calmly walked into the kitchen to brew my coffee.

He followed me into the kitchen and said, "Before you start saying you don't know where she is, I already know she was seeing you every night on a regular basis."

He had a Russian accent, and standing close to him, I could tell he was a strong man by his physique. Though he was tall and lean, he was muscularly toned. I, on the other hand, was not prone to working out at the gym. Despite the situation, I remained calm.

I did not want to insult his intelligence by pretending she was not there, so I asked, "How much would it cost to buy out her debt?"

He wryly smirked, then said, "This one is not for sale, only to rent."

I could tell he was not going to leave without her, and I suddenly became focused on how to prevent this from happening. I surmised I would not prevail in a one on one fight with him as he was much taller than me and in way better shape. I spotted a steak knife in the draining board next to the sink and figured I could harm him enough with that to prevent him from going to the bedroom where Lucy was.

I grabbed the handle, but my body just took over and I thrust the knife straight into his chest. It went completely into him, and he had a bewildered look of shock on his face. He tried to grab hold of the handle with both hands, but I held fast to the knife so that his hands clasped mine. I pushed forward, still holding the knife, and he fell backwards against my kitchen cabinets. As he dropped to the floor, I let go of the knife and stood there over him, as if by some chance he may try to get back up, but he stayed on the floor.

I could not believe what I had just done; it was as if some spirit came over me and made me do it, then flew away, leaving me to figure out what to do next. I was beside myself, not with grief, but astonishment at what I'd done. Did I really just kill another human? I quickly rationalised that I did it to protect Lucy. But seriously, protecting an online call girl from her pimp, what the hell was I thinking? I could always say I stood my ground to a home invader, but having a clandestine lab set up in my house would not help matters from a legal standpoint. What possessed me to take such a drastic measure? I was perplexed at my action, confused as I stood there, in my house, staring at the dead body. A pool of blood was forming around it, and the lack of motion made me dizzy. Nothing around me seemed to move, not the leaves or the branches outside my window. Time had stood still.

I wondered how it came down to this. How did I get myself into this situation? Embracing the situation in front of me, a lifeless body with my steak knife protruding from his chest, something beyond surreal captured me. It was me that had thrust the knife in him. Had it become normal for me to do such a thing? Was this acceptable? I was an educated man who paid his taxes, what the hell was I doing?

I suddenly felt alone, displaced, as if I no longer belonged to this world. My killing another person now constituted damnation. I felt destined to a life of roaming, with no real connection to another soul. I would always carry a pronounced burden of guilt with me. One way or another, I would have to pay for it, but I didn't know how. It wasn't until Lucy ran up to me, arms full of towels, yelling to help her soak up the blood that I snapped out of it.

"Hurry up Paul, before we have to bleach the entire kitchen," she yelled.

Only one thought came into my mind, and that was to call Dan. I had programmed his number into my cell phone, so I pulled it out of my back pocket and called him. I was not even sure what to say to him.

"Hello," he answered after just two rings.

"Dan, this is Paul up the road."

Lucy looked up at me inquisitively while placing the towels up against Dimitri's body. She patted him down and removed his cell phone from his shirt pocket. She also took out his gun which was harnessed to the side of his body.

"Yeah Paul, what can I do for you?"

"I have a big problem down here at the house and I really need some help, can you come over?" I was worried he may say no.

"Sure, I'll be right down," he said before hanging up.

Lucy asked, "Do you think that's a good idea?"

I thought about it for a minute. I was taking a lot of risk calling him. I assumed he had worked for a crooked man before and probably did unscrupulous things while employed by him. Perhaps I was wrong getting him involved in this, but what choice did I have? It was not like I knew what to do with a dead body. Besides, I was a good judge of character, and I trusted my instinct.

A few minutes later, Dan knocked on the door. I greeted him and let him in. I felt relieved that he was there. We walked over to the kitchen.

"What the hell happened here?" he asked obviously concerned.

I didn't want to say I had just killed Lucy's pimp to keep him from taking her back into servitude for fear of embarrassing her, but what choice had I, so that is exactly what I did. I quickly went over the past few weeks, leaving out the details of us making fentanyl together, and hoped he would be empathetic towards us.

Lucy then took Dimitri's cell phone, which she left on, and his gun and went into the bedroom. I knew this was going to go one of two ways. Either Dan was going to help us, or he would call the police.

"I'm going to need you to take that knife out of his chest and then thoroughly clean it in the sink. Then you are going to take every steak knife in the set you have and put them in an unmarked box. You'll need to drop them at a Goodwill drop box. Be sure not to leave any prints. If there happens to be an attendant there, which I doubt, as it's so cold outside, do not have him write you a receipt."

Lucy came back out from the bedroom and was listening to what Dan was saying. He looked at her, then said, "I take it one of the cars in the driveway is his. Is anyone going to be looking for it?"

Lucy spoke up, "I'll take care of it."

"Well don't leave any prints in, or on, the car. I'd suggest leaving it at an airport parking garage." He looked over at me. "I need to get my truck in your driveway."

"I'll move the vehicles out of the way," I said.

Dan left to get his truck while Lucy went out and moved Dimitri's car out to the front yard. His keys had been in his sweater pocket, along with his cell phone. She had also taken out a wad of cash from his front pocket and placed it down her bra.

I parked my car behind Dimitri's out in the yard so Dan could back his truck all the way up the driveway. He arrived with a blue tarp in the truck's back bed. He brought the tarp inside with him and then laid it out next to the body. We then rolled Dimitri into the tarp, wrapped up good and tight. After making sure no one was in sight, we quickly carried him out and then placed his body into the back of Dan's truck. For some odd reason I felt a rush of pleasure come over me, which I could not explain, except for the fact that I was literally, getting away with murder. It felt almost too easy at that moment, and I began to think perhaps there was an unforeseen consequence I would be facing soon.

"Should I ask where you're taking the body?" I asked Dan.

He looked at me with a slightly annoyed glare. "No, you should not. I'll call you later to check in with you, and don't go joy riding all over town in his car. The sooner you get rid of it, the better."

He then got into his truck and slowly drove off. I felt relieved to be rid of the body and felt indebted to Dan for getting rid of it so quickly. I felt that he was very capable of disposing of it properly and someplace where it would not be found.

I went inside to check on Lucy. She had gathered the steak knives and was washing them in the sink. There were six in the set.

"I'll drop these off at the Salvation Army in Saint Lucie. There is an empty shoe box in your closet I can put them in." She looked happy to help.

"Okay," I said, "just make sure there's no receipt in the box."

I looked down at the kitchen floor. It was as if it never happened, except for the dark red hue in the grout where the blood seeped into. I felt like Lucy and I needed to talk about what just happened, but I just couldn't face it. All I really wanted was to move forward and forget about it.

*

The following week I went to work as usual. I wanted to maintain a normal image after what I had done, business as usual, so to speak. Of course, my co-workers were oblivious to what happened, but for some reason, I felt like all eyes were upon me. I became reserved and found it hard to concentrate. Fortunately, the busy pace helped the time go by quickly.

Sara, the lead technician, pulled me aside one afternoon. She had been at the drug store for years and was a very proactive person; she thrived on the busy environment. She also was very in tune with her co-workers, and she could tell something was bothering me.

"Are you alright Paul," she asked me. "You've been quiet these last few days, not your usual self."

Not wanting to tell her what was really bothering me, I told her, "I'm just a little sad with the holidays coming and not having Tricia and her kids to celebrate with."

Sara was aware of the breakup and how devastated I was afterward. I always found it easy to tell her things about my personal life. She was very empathetic about it.

"Aw, I'm sorry," she said. "You can come and have Christmas dinner at my house; the whole family will be there."

She was from a Mexican family. She had three children and her and her husband would always host a big family gathering, between birthdays and holidays. They would usually cook a pig and get a large cake from Publix.

"That is awfully nice of you, but I'll be okay," I told her.

*

It turned out Lucy had a busy week. Using Dimitri's car, she dropped off the set of steak knives to the Salvation Army store. They had a drive through area in the back of the building where people drove up to drop off or pick up items. She simply got out of the car and placed the box on top of a pile of donated items and then left without even being noticed.

She then drove out to the house where the other girls were staying. They were confused as to why Dimitri had not come back. They also were very worried about obtaining their necessities. Lucy knew Igor would be back at the end of the week and did not want the girls in any danger.

"Let me take you girls to the bus station so you can go back home to family or friends," she offered.

"Well what happened to Dimitri," Hailey asked innocently enough.

The other girls were certain something drastic must have happened to him but given Hailey's youth, she did not catch on to that fact. Lucy thought about what to say for a moment. One of the other girls gave her a hug.

"Dimitri won't be coming back," Lucy told her.

They all sat around on the couch together and discussed what to do. They knew they could not stay there, but it was the consensus that they did not want to leave each other. They had strangely fallen into a family of sorts themselves, looking out and caring for each other. Also given their active drug addictions, they really had no desire to go back home as Lucy had suggested.

It was mutually decided upon that they would stay at a local hotel and try to figure something out. Besides, they had steady clientele they saw that could provide them with the necessary income to help support their habits. Knowing the area, Lucy was aware of a motel in Fort Pierce; slightly north of where they were that would be perfect for the time being. She knew the manager there would not ask questions and was prone to looking the other way to certain suspicious or illegal activity.

So, the girls all gathered their belongings along with some snacks that were left over in the kitchen. Lucy went into Dimitri's room and found the safe in the closet. She had an idea of what the combination might be, given past conversations she had with him, and tried it. It opened, and inside she found the stash of heroin along with syringes. She took it out of the safe, and then closed it back up.

They felt funny, all piling into Dimitri's car at the same time, and they chuckled. It was roomy enough to fit them all in, while Lucy drove, after they had thrown their bags into the trunk. It was as if they were going on a field trip or vacation together. Hailey rolled down the window next to her and waved her hands outside. Even though they were all still very much addicted to drugs, for a short while anyway, they felt happy and free.

They got to the hotel, a dingy Motel 6, located between a Flying J truck stop and a McDonalds, right off the interstate. It was a busy street with lots of trucks pulling in and out and people coming to get food or gas. The motel was two stories high and not luxurious. Lucy pulled in and asked the girls to wait in the car while she paid for the rooms. Since they would not have access to transportation, they decided to use one room for their transactions with clients, and then the five of them would share two other rooms.

Lucy walked into the office and saw the manager she was familiar with. "Hola Heath, it's been a while."

"Hola Lucy, it's been a long time." He looked surprised to see her.

Heath was short and stout, with a dark, straggly beard. He looked unkempt and was of a shady character. He was in love with cash, but never seemed to have any. He was a man prone to bad luck and poor judgments. Hence, he continued to work as the manager of the Motel 6. His one good quality was that he never asked questions.

"I need three rooms, all next to each other, and preferably at the end of the hall, can you handle that," she asked, wanting as little interaction with him as possible.

"How many nights?"

"Let's go on a week by week basis," she replied.

"And how will you be paying for this?" He looked at her with a greedy yet predictable face.

She took out the wad of cash she had lifted from Dimitri's pocket and gave it to him. "There's a lot more where this came from," she assured him. Having dealt with him in the past, she knew he would pocket any money she gave him given his seedy nature.

He did not bother to count it but merely looked to see it was all one hundred-dollar bills, and a nice stack of them at that. Of course, he did not register the rooms as taken, but he got the room keys ready and then gave them to Lucy. He wondered about the upcoming ball games this weekend and who he should bet on.

She went back out and gathered the girls. Although considerably less glamorous than their last residence, it was refreshing for them all. They got settled into the rooms, which were on the first floor at the far side away from the office. They left the farthest room down void of their belongings and decided to make that their work room. They also figured they could use it as a sort of living room to watch television in when they were not entertaining clients there. Facing outwards at the back of the hotel, it was out of sight of the main highway, but did overlook the truck stop's parking lot. Lucy looked out of the window and was amazed at the number of semi-trucks that were parked there and how they all backed into their spaces instead of pulling straight in.

Lucy felt sorry that the girls would have to stay in such a bleak place, and she felt responsible for the sudden change of circumstances. She remembered she had the weekly supply of necessities out in the car, so she ran out to get it. It was the least she could do for them, aside from paying for the rooms. She wondered who should be responsible for holding onto it during the week. Knowing addiction, the way she did, she felt it would be almost certain they would use it all up well before they should, being incapable of rationing it. With this concern, she decided to let Hailey ration it out. Even though she was the youngest of the bunch, she was, in Lucy's opinion, the most trustworthy.

She went back around and pulled Hailey aside from the others. "So hey, here's enough stuff to last you and the others a few days, at least until you get yourselves up and running."

Hailey looked surprised, "Well thank you, that is so nice." She smiled at Lucy with appreciation.

"You know you guys are going to have to find another supplier?"

"Yeah, I just don't know exactly where we should look. I really don't want to end up back in the hood part of town again; I thought I left that part of me behind."

Lucy looked at her sympathetically, "Well maybe I can figure something out, let me get back with you."

*

The next day, while I was away at work, Lucy used Dimitri's car to drive down to Miami. She brought all her money with her and then met the lawyer at his office. She had arranged to pay him in cash to get her mother legal status to live in the U.S. and to purchase her a nice condo apartment located off Biscayne Bay. This was all agreed upon during their first meeting, for which he was going to receive a nice bonus, setting Lucy back an even quarter of a million dollars. Being an unscrupulous lawyer, he had a money counting machine set up in the back of his office to make sure it was all there.

He handed her the keys to the condo, along with the signed deed and an identification card he obtained by using another woman that resembled her mother. Knowing the cracks in the system, he had many tricks he used to help people obtain citizenship who could afford the costs of bending the law. He also used the woman to sign all the required documents at the closing. Lucy was happy and thanked him for all his help.

She then drove to her mother's apartment. She had most of her belongings already packed, but Lucy wanted to show her now. She was excited to see the place and the look on her mother's face, but she was also worried that the Russians would know where she was and just wanted to get her mom out of there as quickly as possible.

"Come on mom, we can collect your things later," she said in Spanish. She figured that if they did come looking for her and saw her belongings were still there, they would waste time waiting for her to show back up.

When they got in the car, her mom asked, "Whose car is this, yours?"

"It is now," not trying to sound pretentious, though her mother was not happy with the answer.

They drove to the complex, which looked enormous to them both. It was a vast contrast to where they just came from, and her mother was overwhelmed with joy. They pulled into the below ground parking garage; she already had a parking pass given to her along with the closing documents. Finding their way to the elevator, they made it up to the tenth floor. Not far from the elevator door was apartment, number 1001.

Putting the key into the door, Lucy turned to her mom and said, "We're here."

They went in together, and Lucy's mother looked around in amazement. "It's beautiful Lucienda."

They toured the entire apartment. It was a two-bedroom, one bathroom with spacious views of the bay below. It was much bigger than the ratty apartment she was residing in now. The apartment also came furnished and was ready to move into.

"This is yours, mom," Lucy said smiling.

"I love it." She gave Lucy a big hug.

"Please mom, I don't want you to ever go back to the other place, ever again." Lucy looked at her concerned.

"What about my clothes, dear?"

"It isn't safe I'm afraid," she replied. "It's better to leave those things there and get new things. Promise me you will never go back, okay?" Lucy held her mother by the shoulders, looking her in the eyes while saying this.

Her mother nodded and said, "I understand."

Chapter 10

Inception

That next Friday when I was off from work, we both drove to Saint Lucie West to drop Dimitri's car back off at the house. Lucy thought it best if I did not know exactly which house it was, so I pulled into the gas station parking lot while she drove on into the neighbourhood. I went inside and got us a couple of barbeque sandwiches to eat, then waited for her outside on the bench where we had eaten before.

Soon she came and sat next to me. "Did everything go alright?" I asked.

"Yes, and I left the keys on his dresser."

"And did you check to make sure none of your stuff was left behind?" I asked, just trying to be thorough.

Lucy looked at me in a funny way but could tell I was just concerned. "Everything is out of there, and I even wiped for prints."

"Cool, let's eat," I said relieved and tore into my sandwich.

The next day, Lucy and I made the biggest batch of Fentanyl yet, nearly two hundred grams. Lucy was insistent on making a large quantity and explained that the demand called for it. I thought we should list it as twenty separate packets holding ten grams each, which would yield us two hundred thousand dollars, but Lucy wanted to list it as one bulk sale, having confidence we would have no problem selling it that way. I had never thought of making that kind of money in basically a day's time, and even though we had sold all our other batches rather easily, I still held onto a slight skepticism of selling this batch as quickly.

While Lucy was carefully spreading the still moist powder under the heat lamp, with latex gloves and a surgical mask on, I went and sat down on the bed to check my email. That was when I noticed it, an email from Tricia. I was not expecting one from her, and I had to catch my breath before opening it. She had sent me a few screenshots of some nasty texts I had sent her back when we were arguing. This didn't occur often, but when we did, we would both say and text mean things to each other. At the bottom of the email under the images, she typed "my closure."

I was floored. "Why had she taken the time to even send this to me?" I asked myself. Perhaps she was letting me know she had moved on. I could not understand how it was so easy for her while I was obviously still not over her myself. My emotions were stirred, and I felt slightly sick. The right side of my head began to ache. I felt confined and needed to get out of the house.

I got up and peaked into the other room. "Hey darling, I'm going to head out for a bit and pick up some more supplies."

"Okay, grab us some more chips while you are out," she asked, working on the batch.

"Sure thing," I replied.

I was relieved that she did not want to come along. I needed to clear my head and figure out why the hell Tricia's email rattled my inner equilibrium so profoundly. Besides, we did need more coffee to ship the new batch out in. It was also nice not to have any reservations about leaving Lucy alone with so much product, which was worth more than my house. A partner in crime, so to speak.

*

Igor had not heard from Dimitri all week, which was a little out of the ordinary. He presumed that the girls must have had a busy week, and so he was curious to see what the week's take would be. It was a busy week for him as well. The Mexican cartel had started using fentanyl to increase the potency of their heroin, and many of their clients were asking the organisation for the same. Usually they would cut their drugs with agents to decrease the potency and increase the amount sold to the distributors, a practice used for decades. It seemed that now the Mexican cartel, at least on the eastern seaboard of the United States, were using fentanyl as a cutting agent, which actually increased the heroin's potency, and which gave the drug users on the streets a better high. This created much discussion amongst the Russian syndicate, and even prompted a meeting, set to occur next week, with the head of their narcotics division to be there. Her name was Katrina, and she was known for her quiet demeanor, but deadly tactics. Igor was really looking forward to just spending some time with Dimitri and relieving some of his stress.

When he arrived at the house, Dimitri's car was parked outside, as usual. Igor smiled and shook his head at himself, realising he had been overreacting to the lack of contact from Dimitri. He knocked on the front door, but no one answered. He had a spare key and used it to get inside. All was quiet. None of the girls were in the living room watching television, as was customary when he came there, and he did not see Dimitri anywhere. He walked into the kitchen and saw there were no dirty dishes in the sink. He opened Dimitri's door to his room and saw no one there, then went and checked the three spare bedrooms in the back of the house. All the girls were gone as well.

Igor began to feel frustrated and felt like punching a wall. 'I bet it was that bitch Sky', he thought to himself.

He got out his cell phone and called Dimitri. Perhaps he had taken the girls for a walk somewhere, though he highly doubted it. Then he heard ringing coming from Dimitri's bedroom. He walked in quickly, hoping not to find Dimitri's body lying somewhere on the floor. He saw the cell phone vibrating on the dresser while it rang. He hit the end call on his phone and looked thoroughly around the floors, closet and under the bed. There was no sign of a body or a struggle.

He picked up Dimitri's phone, knowing something bad must have happened, as no one in the syndicate was supposed to be without their designated phone. He knew the passcode because one evening, the topic came up between them, and Dimitri had told him what it was. Dimitri's favorite movie was *Inception*, so he made his code 528491, after the safe combination in the movie. He also liked the fact that none of the numbers were repeated in the combination.

Igor unlocked the phone and saw the missed calls from himself, as well as the few unread text messages he had sent Dimitri. Nothing seemed out of the ordinary, and he wondered how he would be able to find where Dimitri was. He remembered that Dimitri would use his MapQuest app to drive any of the girls to their client's location, and that he was supposed to go fetch Sky from wherever she was last weekend. He clicked on the app and looked up the last address he had searched. It was to an address in Fort Pierce, about thirty minutes away, and it was used the next day after his visit and talk with Dimitri about retrieving her.

He looked over the room again. Everything was in place, nothing ransacked, and the safe was closed. He immediately decided not to hesitate and went out to his car with Dimitri's phone to drive out to the address. He found that his heart was pounding. He had certainly seen his share of violence, and inflicted pain and suffering numerous times before, but this was different. This time it was personal to him.

He arrived at the house around noon. There were no other cars in the driveway, so he pulled in. He checked his gun, then got out and walked up to the door and knocked.

Lucy came out of the back room to go see who it was, half thinking it was Paul, but then saw Igor looking into the front living room window. He spotted her, and then gently tapped on the glass with the end of the barrel.

"Don't make me use this on you," he mouthed at Lucy through the window.

She knew he could easily break down the front door given his size and strength, so she went and unlocked it.

"I knew you had something to do with this whole mystery," he said, walking in.

He closed and locked the door. She looked at him without saying anything and trying not to look nervous. He turned and faced her.

"Where are Dimitri and the other girls?" he asked.

"He's at the hotel with them collecting money," she replied.

"Why would he take them all to a hotel?" Igor asked, not really believing her.

"He said there was a new batch of ladies coming in and he had to make room for them at the house." Lucy tried to maintain her calm.

Igor put his arm around the back of Lucy's neck and began to walk towards the bedrooms with her. His arm felt heavy to her and she knew she could not fight him off. He held onto his gun in the other hand.

"Oh yeah, we will see about that." He had a low Russian accent that annoyed her.

He then raised the gun to Lucy's side, ready to fire it, if need be. He looked in the first spare bedroom which only had a small bed set up in it along with some random boxes sitting on the floor. They went to the back, master bedroom, then looked in the last room with the clandestine lab set up in it.

He looked at the set up with an impressed face, and then he saw the white powder under the heat lamp. He lowered the gun and walked in, leaving Lucy by the entrance. He walked closer to the table to have a look.

"So, this is what you're doing with your spare time," he observed.

Lucy did not speak.

"What are you cooking here, meth?" His eyes looked wide.

"What do you care?" Lucy said defiantly.

Igor quickly walked back towards her and slapped her so hard she fell onto the floor. "Just answer the question, you slut!"

Lucy began to cry and said, "Okay, okay, it's meth." She continued to sob and gave him a glance of defeat.

He smiled, then turned back around to have a closer look. He enjoyed snorting a little cocaine when he was over to see Dimitri. It heightened their senses sexually. He felt the urge to try some, thinking of Dimitri at that moment.

What Igor did not realise was that Dimitri had told Lucy about this late one night. He made her swear to secrecy about the matter. Dimitri loved to hear secrets, as well as tell them. To get him to talk about things, Lucy would often make up false stories about people. It was her way of getting to learn more about Dimitri, Igor, the syndicate, and all their weaknesses.

Igor scooped out a small amount of powder with his pinky finger and tapped it onto the metal table. He looked over at Lucy who was still sitting on the floor, and then took out a large wad of cash from his pocket. He rolled up a fifty-dollar bill into a makeshift straw. He then snorted the powder up into his nostril, expecting to get a nice, quick jolt of energy. But his body almost became limp and he felt as if he were given a tranquilizer instead. He turned around and looked down to Lucy, realising that she had lied to him about what the powder was. It was too late, and he collapsed onto the floor, dead.

*

I got a call from Lucy while at Sam's Club. "Can you hurry back here, something terrible has happened?"

"What's wrong?" I asked.

"Igor found me, somehow. I think you may need to bring that guy Dan back over," she suggested, sounding quite unemotional.

"Oh shit, what happened?" I asked, worried she may have shot him or something.

"I'll tell you about it when you get here," she said.

"Are you okay?" I asked.

"Yeah, I'm okay," she replied and hung up.

I was glad that she wasn't injured and was curious to see what happened. I was also curious to see what this guy Igor looked like. Her telling me that I would need to bring Dan over meant she must have killed the man, unless she was holding him hostage at the house somehow.

I called Dan and asked if he could meet me at my house in an hour, then hurried home. I found Lucy in the kitchen cleaning the beakers and such from our big cook. She looked calm, considering.

"So, where is he?" I asked apprehensively.

"This way." Lucy dried her hands with a dish towel and walked back to the lab room.

I saw Igor lying motionless on the floor. He was bigger than I had pictured him; not as fit as Dimitri to be sure. I squatted near him and looked at his face. He looked like a mean person. There was no blood that I could tell around him.

"How did he die?" I asked, assuming he was dead.

"He took a sniff of the fentanyl thinking it was methamphetamine. He saw the lab back here and thought that was what we were making."

That kind of surprised me. I knew what we were making was potent, but I didn't realise a snort of it was lethal. That made me a little nervous as the last thing I wanted was to accidentally overdose on any of it.

Then I glanced up to her. "Well how the hell did he find you?"

"I don't know. Dimitri must have told him about you being a regular client of mine and how he must have thought this is where I would be."

I stood up, "Well do you think he told anyone else?"

"Igor would have been the only person he would have said anything to about us." She stood there innocently enough and started to look upset.

I decided not to push the matter any further and looked at the body again. "Well, he is going to be a pain in the ass to move, that's for sure."

We both were stirred by a knock on the front door. I looked at Lucy, who looked straight back at me. Then I remembered I had called and asked Dan to come over.

"That must be Dan," I reassured her.

I peeked out of the living room window to make sure there were no cop cars out front. Then I saw Dan standing by the front door, so I let him inside. This time, he had black leather gloves on.

"Hello Dan, thanks for coming over so quickly."

"Yeah yeah," he answered back, sounding annoyed. "I see you have a different vehicle in the driveway today."

I smirked and motioned for him to follow me. We went back to the room where Igor was. Dan scanned over the room. I had not told him about the little operation going on here yet. He now had a full mental picture of our lab. Lucy stood off to the side, remaining quiet.

"You know it's none of my business, but you may want to consider moving your little clandestine lab to a rental property or storage site." He seemed more concerned about that than the dead body lying on the floor. He then looked down at Igor, "Are you two expecting any more 'unwanted' visitors?"

I looked over to Lucy and said, "I surely hope not."

"Well, you are going to want to get rid of this car quicker than the last one; I noticed it lingering around most of the week." He looked at both of us with an unsatisfactory glance. "I can see he's not bleeding out all over the floor so there's no need to move him right now given that it's broad daylight out."

For some reason Tricia's email came to mind, and I said, "Let's put him behind the wheel of his car and drive it off the road someplace." I was still reeling from it. For some reason, the thought of her and our ended relationship made me want to do something careless and haphazard.

Dan looked at me like I was crazy, saying, "Yeah, let's dispose of that very idea right now."

"Why?" I persisted, "It'll look like he fell asleep at the wheel after using drugs."

Dan gave me a cold look. "All it takes is one witness seeing you get out of the car and into another, or even a video traffic recorder catching you on tape."

"Okay, well give me a little bit to get my thoughts in order," I told him. I motioned for him to come out of the bedroom. He did not seem to be in as much of a hurry to get rid of this body as he was with Dimitri, I'm assuming, since there was no blood seeping out onto the floor. The fact that Igor was much larger and would be harder to carry outside unnoticed probably had something to do with that as well.

"Can I have a word," he asked, while walking out with me.

We went outside and I closed the front door. It was another chilly day out, and I was eager to get back inside. I noticed the tree branches swaying from the wind.

He started, "I don't know what you're into, although I have a pretty good idea, but that last gentleman you had me dispose of looked like a Russian gangster, and if I had to guess, so does the man in your house now. If you are 'offing' certain people of a syndicate, it's only a matter of time before they send more than one guy."

I contemplated what he said for a moment. "I hear you. Speaking of which, I need to pay you for your help."

"You can take care of that when I come back. What I think you should do right now is talk to your partner in there. Do you know who she is exactly?" He looked at me intently.

I thought about this also and then replied, "I thought so anyway."

"I also think you should talk to Josh across from my house. He can hook you up with some chemicals to dissolve the blood left on your kitchen floor."

"You mean the guy that works for the sheriff's department?" I asked, concerned.

"Yes, he is good people and most importantly, can be trusted. He's only a crime scene technician, not a sheriff's officer. Come on down with me now and I'll introduce you."

I was surprised he would recommend someone affiliated with law enforcement, but I trusted his judgement.

"Sure, why not, just give me one second." I ran back inside the house and grabbed a ten-thousand-dollar stack of twenties I had set aside for him in my sock drawer. I figured that was a fair amount of money to give him for what he had done for us. On the way back out, I told Lucy I had to take care of something with Dan and would be back shortly. I went back out and handed it to him, "Here you go, for the last favor."

"Thank you." He noticed the wrapper denoting ten thousand dollars on it and seemed content. He placed it inside his coat pocket, and we proceeded to walk up the block together.

When we got there, Dan took off his gloves and knocked on the door. The house was older, like mine, built in the seventies. The yard was a little disheveled with clutter and weeds. Josh opened the door, a jumpy young man in his late twenties, tall and lanky with a touch of premature baldness.

"Hey Josh, this is my friend I told you about that lives just up the road from us." He gave Josh a glance and nodded at him.

Josh's eyes lit up, "Oh yeah, come in, come in." He waved us in, excited to have company. "I just made some coffee, would you like a cup?"

"No thank you," I said, "I just had a cup."

We both walked in and Josh closed the door. Dan and I moseyed on into the living room. I could see Josh pouring a cup of coffee from a regular coffee brewer. I was surprised that someone his age would brew coffee, given everyone I knew had a Keurig.

"So, Paul here has a little blood stain problem in some unsealed grout, what do you suggest he do?" Dan had waved no to coffee.

I looked around while standing there. It was a cluttered house with books and magazines lying around in various places. The furniture was mostly made of wood and looked homemade. Various little projects were started, and I got the impression Josh liked to stay busy, but also, was easily distracted.

Josh walked over to his couch, took a sip of coffee, and thought for a few seconds. "Well, the main thing with unwanted blood that is left behind is destroying the DNA in it, so it can't link you to the victim."

He sat down and got comfortable. I was impressed with how cool he was about the subject, almost nonchalant. I wondered just how much Dan had told him about me. I also thought it strange just how accepting he was of the situation. I realised he must have seen many gruesome crime scenes, but not wanting to report me to the authorities, kind of made me wonder. Perhaps he was just in need of some extra income, as I knew crime scene technicians were not highly paid.

"The first thing you'll want to do is thoroughly wipe the area down with bleach-soaked paper towels. Some people use bath towels, but I wouldn't recommend that. No one would think twice about a garbage bag full of dirty paper towels, whereas a bag full of bath towels looks incriminating. Plus, paper towels weigh much less."

At this point, Dan said, "Well, I'm going to leave you two to it," and turned to walk towards the door.

"Let me call you about that other problem in a little while," I shouted at him.

Dan turned his head around and gave me an unimpressed look, knowing I really wanted to carry out my plan of driving Igor off the road someplace.

Josh continued, having not paid attention to Dan, but relished in his thoughts. "You'll need oxygenated bleach to destroy the DNA. I can make it for you, I'm pretty sure I have some sodium percarbonate lying around somewhere, and it wouldn't take long either."

"I'd be most grateful," I said, insinuating that I would pay him well for his effort and discretion.

"Of course," he said, "and after that, you will want to be quite thorough by scrubbing the area with a solution of baking soda and peroxide. This may brighten the grout area considerably, but damn if a crime scene investigator could find any viable blood, even someone as good as me."

We both laughed. I could have stayed longer, as Josh seemed in no hurry to have me leave, but I was anxious to get back and see Lucy. We exchanged phone numbers and he said he would get started on my cleaning solution.

Before leaving I asked, "Do you investigate many drug overdoses where the person was driving at the time?"

He looked at me inquisitively and said, "No, not that I can recall."

I hoped not to arouse suspicion from him, as I was set in my idea of doing exactly that with Igor. That is, if Dan didn't remove the body before I got the chance. I wondered if Josh would be called out to the scene after I did so.

On my way back, I stopped at George's house, which was only two houses down from Josh's. I knocked on his door and Cassie started yapping inside. I could hear George scalding her as he approached the door.

When he opened the door, he smiled. "Oh, hey Paul, how are you?"

He stepped out and closed the door behind him to keep Cassie from coming out. I caught a glimpse of her tail wagging when he did. She sure was an adorable little dog.

"I'm doing okay, thanks. Say, I have a silly question for you. Do you think they installed any traffic cameras between here and the next exit south off the interstate recently?"

The county had just widened and paved Indrio Road which was the main highway that ran from the interstate all the way east to the Intracoastal Waterway. Our development was located at the halfway point. Though there were only a couple of intersections between where we were and the interstate, I was not sure if they had installed video cameras at the new intersections. I felt that George would know since he had installed all the fiber optics on Jupiter Island. The last thing I wanted would be a detective accessing the video surveillance cameras if I did carry out my plan.

"Well," he said, "there's only one way to find out. Let's take a drive and see. We need to get out of the house for a bit; we can take my car."

"Oh, I don't want to put you out like that," I said worried.

"No problem at all, just let me get my keys." He went back into the house, then came out holding Cassie. "She goes with me everywhere nowadays."

I smiled and we all got into his car, Cassie occupying the back seat. She was excited and her tail was wagging vigorously. I sat down in the front passenger seat and patted Cassie on her head. She seemed to enjoy the extra attention.

George got us out to Indrio Road, and we headed west toward the interstate. "They sure did a nice job with this road. I heard they are bringing a Publix supermarket out here soon."

"Oh really, I didn't know that," I replied.

The area was underdeveloped in comparison to Palm Beach County where I had just moved from. It somewhat reminded me of what my hometown of Jupiter was like growing up. It was airy and the people were friendly and laid back.

George pointed to the four corners of the intersection we had stopped at. "No video cameras," he confirmed.

"What about those?" I pointed to the white objects on top of each light pole that looked like cameras.

"Those are traffic sensors, not video cameras." He smiled over at me. "That is what helps signal the lights to change when you're waiting to turn."

"Oh," I laughed, "they look just like video cameras."

We drove all the way westward to the interstate, then turned around and came back. Cassie was excited, and she often stood up against the back door to look out of the window. Her tail was wagging the whole time we were driving.

"It's a good thing we don't have any banks on this road, or every intersection would have closed circuit cameras mounted," he informed me.

"Yes, good thing." This just confirmed my intention to drive Dimitri's car with him in it and dump it somewhere.

When we got back into his driveway, I thanked him. Cassie ran across the street and went to the bathroom. I could tell George was itching for something to do. Perhaps he was bored.

"Hey George, would you be interested in designing a small retail website for me? Something like eBay but on a much smaller scale; like an individual retail site."

I was not sure if he would want to take on such a responsibility, but he looked excited when I asked him. "Sure, I would love to," he confirmed.

"Of course, I would pay you for it. Give me a few days and we can sit down to discuss it further."

"Okay Paul, I look forward to it." He called Cassie in and we parted ways.

I got back to the house to find Lucy making a sandwich. I remembered she had told me she was hungry when I left earlier, but I hadn't bought anything to bring home. Yet I thought it was an odd thing for someone to be doing while there was a dead body in the house, unless it was something they were used to being around. The thought put chills down my spine, but I brushed it off.

"So, let's do it," I said, walking up to her. "Let's put his ass in the car and drive it off the road somewhere. You can follow me."

"I like it," she said, smiling mischievously.

She took hold of my hand and led me to our room, leaving her sandwich on the counter. On the way, she shut the door to the lab room where Igor's lifeless body lay. We both got undressed in a hurry. It felt like we were doing something wrong and getting a rush from it. Did it seem strange, knowing there was a dead man in the next room? Yes, but I didn't care. We looked at each other for a moment, standing there naked, facing one another. Then we started kissing and jumped into bed. We went at it for over an hour, and I felt alive! Again, I got that feeling of guilty pleasure having done something most people would not even think of, having sex while there was a dead body in the other room. Perhaps I was a sociopath and didn't realise it?

After we finished, she asked "How do you like being a pharmacist?"

"Eh, it's okay. It's a job," I replied.

"You sound unimpressed. Don't you enjoy what you do?" she continued.

I chuckled, "Most of the time I'm counting pills five at a time; not very stimulating."

She looked surprised. "Well still, you have to be very smart to be a pharmacist. You have to know the names of all the drugs and what they all do. Isn't it confusing? I know I wouldn't be able to memorise all of those medications."

"In retail pharmacy, it is mostly about getting the scripts filled and out to the patient as quickly as possible. There isn't much brain work involved."

"Don't you have to know if certain drugs interact with each other and stuff like that?" She seemed surprised by my lack of enthusiasm for my work.

"Yes, but they have programmes now that catch all of that for us. We are just there to sign off on everything and fill as many scripts as possible," I explained.

"At least it pays well," she replied.

I smirked and said, "Not as well as selling fentanyl."

We both soon fell asleep and did not wake up until almost three in the morning. At first, I sat up startled, knowing we had to take care of something. I struggled in my thoughts to remember what it was, then it hit me.

"Hey, hey, we have to get up and take care of Igor." I lightly tapped on her shoulder. I wondered if Dan had come by while we were sleeping.

"Oh shit, yeah," she said, half asleep.

We both got dressed and then opened the lab room door. He still lay there on the floor, just looking stiffer. We each grabbed a shoe and began to drag him outside. Luckily, rigor mortis had not yet begun, so we could move the body easily, despite his weight. His car was in the driveway still. Being so dark and late at night, we did not seem to worry about any unwanted onlookers seeing us.

"How are you going to drive it," she asked.

"I'll just sit in his lap," I responded, and she looked at me questionably.

Taking a little time, we got him positioned into the driver's seat. She gave me his keys to the car, and I sat down in Igor's lap. I had to position the seat further back, so I was not right on top of the steering wheel. It felt strange sitting on top of a dead person. She had to close the door for me. I truly began to think I was demented.

"Be careful," she told me from outside the car. "I'll follow right behind you."

She went and jumped into my car, which was parked in the front yard, and waited for me to pull out. I found it difficult to reach the pedals, and when I backed out, I had to come to a sudden halt by stomping on the break. I realised this was going to be a little harder than I thought.

"Thank goodness I only have to go in reverse once," I told myself.

Once we started going straight, it became easier. Lucy followed behind me. We headed to Indrio Road and then west towards the interstate; just as I had done earlier with George. The roads were deserted, and I hoped we would not come across any patrol cars on the way. We both got onto the interstate and proceeded south. There were several miles before the next exit, and I had planned on slowly driving his car off the road somewhere along the way.

But something came over me. I began to wonder what the hell I was doing. Had I lost all sensibility? Perhaps Dan was right? Maybe this was not such a good idea? I wondered if I should return to the house. I kept on driving and was quickly approaching the next exit. Being tired, I closed my eyes tightly for a second, and in the darkness, Tricia's email message appeared much like a backdrop on a dark chalk board.

"Closure" she had put in the email. What the fuck? I became incensed and picked up the speed.

Before I knew it, I was at the next exit, which forked east and west. The west exit was pretty level and came up onto a truck stop where truckers could cross over from the interstate to the turnpike. The east exit, however, required a sharp curve along a steep embankment. The curve declined back under the interstate and off into the city. I knew the exit well, having to take it each day I travelled to work.

Instead of slowing down and taking the curve, I drove straight forward and off the ramp. It was an almost straight drop down of about fifty feet or so. I was not able to fit the seat belt around me since Igor was so large, but I didn't care. I had several seconds of hang time in the air before landing in the grass below. I took my foot off the gas and leaned my body towards the passenger seat, but the bounce of the car upon impact caused the front airbags to deploy, knocking me unconscious.

The next thing I remembered was Lucy knocking on the passenger window and shouting my name. She must have taken the curve all the way under the interstate, made a U-turn, and then turned left onto the on ramp, which ran alongside the area where I had landed. It only felt like a few seconds that I was out, but I was not entirely sure.

Lucy then opened the passenger door and laughed. "What the hell was that Paul? That was fucking awesome!"

She seemed rather impressed with my foolish stunt. I crawled out of the open passenger side, leaving Igor's body still sitting in the driver's seat. Lucy closed the door behind me and helped walk me to our car. I looked around and did not see a single car, which relieved me. We both got in my car, her sitting in the driver's seat, and off we went. I took another last look and still saw no one approaching. Mission accomplished!

Chapter 11

The Fee Bees

The next afternoon, Josh came by with the supplies I needed to scrub out any DNA leftover from Dimitri's blood. I let him in, so he could get a look at the floor area and to pay him. Instead of explaining how to do it, he wound up cleaning the entire kitchen floor and surrounding baseboard area. I was glad, as my head hurt slightly from being knocked unconscious the day before. I noticed that he preferred to do the actual work himself and explain what he was doing in the process. He was full of energy.

When he was finished, he said, "Now sir, I assure you that your house is no longer a crime scene."

I laughed to myself, thinking of the clandestine lab in the back bedroom. "Thank you, Josh, that is a load off my mind."

I motioned for him to come relax over on the couch. "Would you like something to drink?" I asked him.

"I'll take a coffee, black if you have one."

"Of course."

I was amazed that he was able to drink so much coffee, as high energised as he was, not to mention his younger age. I turned on my Keurig and then went to my bedroom to grab him some cash. Lucy was asleep on the bed. I grabbed ten thousand dollars in twenties and split it in half.

I made him a cup of Kenya Highlands by Green Mountain Roasters. I had seen them discuss its great quality on the *Today Show* one morning, and once I tried it, I never drank anything else. For a medium roast coffee, it had one hell of a kick. I was curious to see if it would have any effect on Josh.

"Here you go my friend," and I gave him the cup of coffee along with the five thousand or so in twenties. It just seemed like the right amount to give him for what he contributed.

"Thank you," he said. "That is very generous of you." He did not bother to count it and I assumed that Dan had told him I would not rip him off.

"Think nothing of it," I said gratefully.

"By the way," Josh began, "I was called out to a crime scene early this morning. A man overdosed on opiates and drove his car off the ramp coming off the interstate in Fort Pierce. That in itself, is not too disturbing, but the fact that he is a suspected Russian mobster is. They had me photograph the scene, but the FBI have been called in to lead the investigation. Just thought you would like to know."

I was pretty sure he had a good inclination I was involved, since I had asked him about people overdosing while driving their vehicles just yesterday. He did not go any further than that, just drank his coffee. I did not want to look too obvious, but my curiosity got the best of me.

"Any leads?" I asked.

"Not so much that I've heard," he confirmed, "but they will do an autopsy. His car got towed to the local sheriff's evidence lot. I will keep an ear out for you though."

"Thank you," I acknowledged. Then, I took out the other half stack of twenties that were in my back pocket and gave it to him.

"For your troubles," I told him.

His eyes glowed. "Thank you."

He quickly finished his coffee. "Man, that is really good."

"Isn't it though?" I said.

We said goodbye. I was glad Lucy and I were listing our big batch today, as I had been spending a lot in cash. The cost of doing this kind of business, I thought to myself.

Lucy had shown me several methods of moving cash around that I was not privy to before. The most common way was using Western Union, which allows a person to transfer a maximum of five thousand dollars in any given one-day period. But she also showed me some more obscure ways, which included Popmoney, Zelle, Venmo and CashApp. These were all mobile apps used to transfer money easily around to different accounts or people. She had also set up a dummy account on PayPal called Snow White Cleaning. This allowed her to bill me for cleaning services rendered, and I was able to transfer funds from my bank account to her PayPal account. This all made the movement of funds easier and look legitimate. I was surprised just how savvy she was at all of this.

She also introduced me to TextNow, which was a free phone app that assigned you a local phone number without having to sign up for a phone plan. With this app, we could safely text or call each other, without fear of being monitored by the Feds. We just needed to be signed into a Wi-Fi service. With so many stores and restaurants offering free Wi-Fi, it made it virtually impossible for law enforcement to track.

Once Lucy got up, we went ahead and listed the batch. I ordered us a pizza and we decided not to check the listing again until we had finished eating. We sat down together and watched another movie, this time *The Departed*. She really enjoyed it, though she cheered for Jack Nicholson's character and was upset when he died near the end. I would play with her at times, pretending I wanted to check on the listing, trying to slide the laptop over to myself. She would slap my hands when I did so, and then I would slide it back.

Finally, after we had finished the movie, we checked our listing. It had sold, and again it was going down to our Miami customer. I was pleasantly surprised, while Lucy seemed to have anticipated it. The website still got a good cut as they charged a percentage of the sale. This bothered me very much and made me want to start our own site so we would not have to pay fees.

"The eBay of the dark web," I commented to Lucy, smirking while I said it.

This time instead of using coffee to ship it, Lucy bought a big bag of Doritos. She opened the bag up, left the chips inside, and put the bag of fentanyl inside, using latex gloves. Then she resealed the bag using a thin amount of cement glue. Again, I was impressed with her imagination and ingenuity. She put the Doritos bag in a box and shipped it out the next day. As was customary, the site held onto our funds for the next twenty-four hours.

I had gone to work as usual, and when I got home, Lucy was in a panic. "I can't access the website!"

"Well I'm sure it's just a computer glitch," I reassured her.

"I don't know. I got a call from Hailey, one of the girls I used to room with, and she said the FBI had shut down the site the girls use today, and now I'm worried."

I could tell from her urgency that she had not transferred our proceeds into the Bitstamp account yet. I jumped onto my cell phone and tried to pull up the site that I'd contacted Lucy on. It was no use; a white page came up with the FBI logo in the background along with a short paragraph.

I squinted at it and read what it said to Lucy, "It says that your site and affiliated websites have been seized."

"Yeah, my girlfriends aren't sure how they will advertise their services now," she replied.

"Well I'm sure the bulk of their income is in cash. We have almost two hundred thousand dollars in Bitcoin tied up on the site!" I was becoming frustrated very quickly.

I rebooted the laptop and jumped onto the Onion browser, then went to the website but it was down too, with the same thing coming up about the FBI. I felt a slight panic come over me.

"And you already mailed out the product?" I asked her.

She looked at me funny. "Ah, yeah," she said.

"Well that's going to create a bit of a crisis for us. I guess I can't call the 'fee bees' for our money," I said half-jokingly.

"You don't think they will be able to track our account back to us somehow, do you?" she asked.

"Well I don't credit the FBI with an overabundance of brains, but it might be prudent to move our lab out of the house, like Dan recommended."

Lucy thought about this for a few moments while I checked online to see if I could find out any further information about the site. That's when I saw a breaking news article about the arrest of the founder, occurring of all places, in a public library. It seems the FBI had learned he was using public internet locations such as Starbucks and the local library to conduct online business matters in relation to the website we were using. Two agents, a man, and a woman, staged a lover's quarrel behind him while he was online on his laptop. This served to distract him, and they were able to confiscate his computer while the screen was still open and unlocked. He was taken into custody without incident and the website was shut down.

I shared this with Lucy. "Well, that answers my question; I think we need to move our lab away from the house."

"Any ideas where to?" she asked.

"Not sure yet, but I'll ask Dan. I was also thinking of starting our own website to sell our product, what do you think?"

"I think that is an awesome idea," she seemed to gleam when saying that.

"Really, I wasn't sure if you would like the idea."

"I love the idea, what are you talking about."

"Well I'm glad to hear it," I said, relieved.

"Say, do you mind if I take the car and go check on the girls?"

"No, of course not. Drive safe."

I handed her the keys to the car and she left. I wrapped my head around the fact that we were essentially out our two hundred thousand dollars and decided to go see George. It was time to start our own website. I wanted to use the same premise as the site we had been using, but to only sell our product and not add other sellers. It was my belief that the Feds were eager to catch the founder because of all the untaxed money he was making from the site, millions of dollars, I assumed. I felt bad for the man, as he was educated, holding two degrees; he just became greedy. If we were able to sell only what we produced, and perhaps hide the origin of the site properly, it could prove profitable enough, without catching the eye of the FBI.

So, I walked down and knocked on George's front door. Again, I could hear Cassie barking, sounding excited.

I was wondering how I could explain to George the concept of our site, with the desire for total anonymity.

He opened the door, and Cassie ran out to me, with her tail wagging. I guess she was getting used to me. "Say, I'd like to discuss the website I had in mind if you have a minute."

"Sure," he said, and he let me inside. Cassie followed behind me.

His house was neater than Josh's, but dimly lit. It looked like it was also built in the seventies. We walked past the living room and into a back room that was adjacent to the kitchen. It had a small table with four chairs around it, and we sat down there.

"Would you like a drink," he asked while pouring himself a glass of whiskey.

I noticed he had a wide selection of alcohol with a sort of mini bar set up along his partition between the kitchen and dining room. "I'll take one of what you're having."

He poured me a whiskey over ice and then sat down across from me. I noticed he had some pictures of him with what looked to be his wife and daughter. The daughter looked to be about ten years old at the time, and the pictures seemed to be from some time ago.

"Is your family home?" I asked, more out of curiosity than prudence.

"My wife and daughter were killed in an automobile accident several years ago," he replied plainly, then took a sip of his whiskey.

"Oh, I'm sorry to hear that," I said, ashamed that I'd asked him.

It occurred to me that this backroom may be his drinking room, where he would sit and ponder what life would be like if his family were still alive. I wondered if he was driving the vehicle they were in at the time, and if he had been drinking. Perhaps he was very lonely and depressed. I wondered why he had never remarried. My mind raced with assumptions, ideas, and questions.

"So, what is this website you have in mind," he asked.

"Well, I want to start a small site that runs on the Tor browser so I can keep my anonymity. You with me so far?" I was fairly sure he would be familiar with the dark web, but I wasn't certain.

"I follow you," he said, unhesitant.

I took a drink, feeling somewhat relieved. "And I want the site to look as if it is based in China, complete with Chinese writing and English subtitles."

"Okay," and he got up to refill his glass.

"On the site, I will be selling certain items, but I don't want other sellers, only myself."

He sat back down. "How many different items will you be selling at any given time?" He sipped his whiskey looking at me intently.

I thought about this for a moment. I doubted we would be able to sell a bulk quantity given the site was new, but I could not be sure. I figured we could always break it down into one-gram bags if the need arose.

"Up to ten or so items at the most. I'll need the ability to upload pictures onto the site and be able to type the description in both Chinese and English. All payments and transactions are to be made through Bitcoin."

"So, I take it you won't be advertising this site on Google," he said.

"Precisely. I have no idea how to start a website with a fake VPN, let alone write code to develop the site," I added.

"I'll need to know what you want to call the site so I can register a domain name," George told me.

"I've been having a think about that and I'd like to call it Moon Lee," I replied. I had always liked that name and it was obviously of a Chinese origin.

"No problem, that should be easy to do," George replied. "I think I can have something you'll like within a week," he confirmed, undaunted.

"A week," I said surprised, "is that all you'll need?"

He smiled and nodded. I petted Cassie, who was sitting on the floor between us. She panted with approval when I did so.

I put an envelope with ten thousand dollars on the table by George, confirming, "For any expenses you might incur."

"Thank you, that is very nice," he replied with a smile.

We both finished our drinks and then he walked me to the door. "Come see me in a week."

"You got it," I replied enthusiastically.

I gave Cassie a pat and she seemed to smile while wagging her tail. I then went over to Dan's house two doors down and across the street. I wanted to get some input from him about where we should move the lab to. I hadn't called first, but his truck was in the driveway. I walked up and knocked on his door. A few moments later, he came and opened the door. Seeing me stand there, he then turned back in his house leaving the door open for me to come in. I walked in and closed the door behind me.

"You know your little stunt made the local news?" he said to me, sounding annoyed.

"I don't watch the news," I said with some degree of sarcasm.

"Well, our mutual friend, Josh told me they called in the FBI to investigate. Did you know that?"

"He mentioned it," I responded.

"You don't seem too worried about it." He looked at me like a disappointed teacher would look at you after you'd failed a test that they would have thought you could pass with ease.

"Should I be?" I asked.

"Well, it's the FBI, not some local working stiff. They are a national organization, you realise?" He seemed bewildered at my lack of concern.

I became a little irritated. "It's the fee bees for crying out loud, not the CIA!"

"Yes, and right now they are conducting an autopsy on your friend, as well as combing through his car for DNA." He looked at me with a scolding glare.

"I didn't leave any," I said confidently.

"And you're sure of that, how?" he asked.

I sighed, remembering I had been knocked unconscious before Lucy had reached me. "Okay, okay, what do you want me to do?"

"I want you to take my advice next time," he insisted.

"I don't plan on there being a next time," I said.

"Ah huh," he remarked doubtfully. "Have you ever been arrested?"

"No, why?"

"I'm just curious if you have ever had a cheek swab for DNA, that's why."

That possibility never had crossed my mind. "No, I haven't," I confirmed.

"Okay, well that's good. It will take a couple of weeks for them to get the lab results from his drug screen, so that buys you some time to move your lab out of the house. I know a guy who owns an outdoor storage facility with no camera surveillance on the property. It's a perfect spot for your needs."

I began to feel like this whole undertaking was turning into a difficult project, and I felt a little discouraged. Perhaps this was becoming too complicated, what with the website being shut down? Not to mention Russian mobsters trying to kill Lucy and myself.

Dan looked at me and said, "Relax, you'll be fine. I'll write the address down. The owner likes cash and asks no questions. The place is close by and his name is Jake."

He ripped out a sheet of paper from a small notebook and wrote down the information for me. I thanked him and assured him I would go to see the man soon. I then went back home to wait for Lucy. She had been gone for some time now, but I knew she had gotten close to some of the girls, so it wasn't a big deal.

*

Lucy pulled into the Motel 6 parking lot. She took a deep breath, not really wanting to see Heath again. She headed into the office. As usual, he was there manning the desk. He looked unkempt with his greasy dark hair and he had not shaved for several days.

He saw Lucy come in and commented, "Quite the bunch of girls you've got here."

Lucy guessed that he would want her to make an introduction, but she just wanted to hurry up and get out of the office and away from him. "Yeah, yeah. How much do I owe you for the week?"

He gave her a wry smile and then leaned comfortably onto the counter. "You know they are all very pretty, but none of them are as beautiful as you. When are we going to tango, lovely?"

Lucy felt somewhat repulsed and wanted to spit in his face. Telling him to "fuck off" would bring her some satisfaction as well, but she knew he was doing her a favor letting her friends stay there, doing what it was they were doing. So, she set aside her impulses and played the flirt.

"You're so bad Heath." She came forward and lightly stroked his forearm. "This is for the next two weeks." She placed a stack of several hundred-dollar bills on the counter in front of him.

He looked down at it and said, "You know you wouldn't have to pay me if you would just let me have a taste."

She was growing tired of his boring advances. "Maybe next time, lover boy."

She turned and walked out before he had a chance to say anything else. He smirked, disappointed at his lost opportunity, but snatched up the stack of hundreds she had left behind for him. Lucy knew he wanted the cash more than the sex. As was usual with him, Heath pocketed the money and did not record it on the books for the owners, who lived out of town.

She walked around the motel and down to where the girls were staying. She looked out onto the truck stop. Many of the truckers who were on their forced thirty-six hour reset would come over to stay at the hotel so they could get in a nice shower and sleep on a full sized bed instead of the bunk most semi-trucks came equipped with. It was a quiet and affordable place for them to go.

She knocked on one of the doors and Hailey answered. "Hey there, it's me."

Hailey came out and gave her a big hug. "It's so nice to see you."

"Where are the others," Lucy asked.

"They are in the next room watching a movie. I just felt like reading, so I stayed in here."

"That's fine. I have some things for you girls."

Lucy had stopped at a pharmacy and bought a box of syringes for them, telling the pharmacist she had a diabetic cat. She also had purchased them a carton of cigarettes and a gallon of milk, which they could empty and use to store their used syringes. She also got them several lighters as well. She gave Hailey all the items and then took out a stuffed zip-lock bag full of fentanyl filled capsules.

Lucy had purchased the empty gelatin capsules online and used baking soda to cut the potency of the fentanyl way down so the girls could use it safely. She then carefully filled up the empty capsules with the diluted powder with the intent of giving them to the girls. She would take care of all of this while Paul was away at work, keeping him out of the loop.

Hailey's eyes lit up. "Oh wow. Is that what I think it is, Lucy? You are such a lifesaver!"

Lucy did not want to tell her that it wasn't heroin, that it was stronger. Her intention was to get them even more dependent on her and her supplies. She figured they would notice her stuff was stronger than any of the local drug dealers, and hence, would pay out more money for it. But she also did it out of a feeling of obligation to them, for it was because of her that they were now in this motel and away from their Russian suppliers. Plus, she had grown to know them, personally, while staying with them at the house in Port Saint Lucie.

"Did you guys save any money from your clients this week," Lucy asked.

"Just a little. It has slowed up since they shut down our site." Hailey went to one of the dresser drawers and pulled out an envelope with some cash in it, which was buried under some clothes. She handed it over to Lucy.

Lucy put it inside her bag, then said, "Come on, let's go talk to the others."

They walked out and over to the other room next door. The other four girls were all comfortably watching some movie on the Hallmark channel. The room was thick with cigarette smoke.

"Hey Lucy," one of the girls said.

They all got up and each one came over to hug her. One of the girls turned off the television, and they all looked glad to see her. Lucy took out a smoke and lit it.

"So, how is everyone?" she asked.

"A little bored. Business has died since they took down the website," the same girl said.

"Well what are you going to do for advertising," Lucy asked.

The same girl spoke up, "Oh, I'm sure another site will pop up."

"Well in the meantime, I paid for your rooms for another week. Perhaps you should work with your regular customers. If you kept their contact numbers, you could text them and see if they would like another encounter."

The girls nodded in agreement.

Lucy continued, "If things get too quiet, take a stroll around the parking lot at the truck stop next door. Just wait until dark before you do so."

"Oh man, I hate truckers," another girl said, "they all smell sweaty."

"Well you have to do what you have to," Lucy retorted.

They all nodded again.

"Okay girls, I have to get going."

"Oh Lucy, you just got here," Hailey said.

"I know, but I'll be back, I promise."

One by one, they all gave her a hug goodbye. Lucy felt bad for them, and she did not want to take over the role as their madam of sorts. She felt like she had inherited the responsibility of keeping them comfortable for now, at least until they were out of danger from the syndicate. She had struck at the Russians first, but she knew they would strike back. The question was how and how quickly. She did not want any of the girls to get caught up in her personal battle with the syndicate, so she felt it was her duty to keep them out of sight from them. She hoped that the violence to come would not entangle them, especially Hailey.

Chapter 12

All Natural

That next weekend, Lucy and I went to check out the storage facility Dan had told me about. It was right off King's Highway, a road used by many truckers that connected Fort Pierce to Vero Beach, so there was lots of traffic. We turned in the main drive, which quickly turned into a dirt road. As we proceeded slowly, the trees and shrubs grew thick so that by the time we approached the storage sheds, we could not even see any cars off the highway. There was no security gate at the entrance, nor any video cameras to be seen. The storage units were nothing more than eight conjoined sheds, four on each side. The four units that faced north were adjacent from a dilapidated house that was made of wood. The gravel driveway ran up to these units and that was where we parked. I looked at Lucy, who stared back at me with a questionable look.

"Hey, at least we know we won't have much company out here," I said reassuringly.

We got out and took in our surroundings. The units were painted a light blue and had white aluminum doors that you had to slide upward to open, much like a garage door. The other four units were facing south and faced nothing but trees and shrubs. The whole complex looked secluded and I wondered how the owner could stay in business. I gathered that he must have inherited the land and probably did not have to pay a mortgage, which would be nice since the property was on at least five acres of land.

Just then, a man emerged from the house and said, "Can I help you?"

The screen door to the front of the house squeaked as it closed. He had a covered porch that was all made of wood and was unpainted. He walked down the wooden steps and over towards us. He was a short man who wore glasses and looked very much like the actor Danny DeVito.

"Yes, hello, are you Jake?" I asked him.

"Yes, I am," he replied and extended his right hand.

"Our good friend Dan highly recommended your storage facility, so we came out to have a look," I explained.

"Oh excellent, Dan is one of the good people. Well as you can see, these are it." He pointed over to the eight units.

He did not seem too concerned about making a sale or getting a commitment to rent, which made me feel comfortable. He also seemed unrushed and did not mind the intrusion, but I could tell he was used to it being quiet. I doubted if he got more than one inquiry a month.

"Well, we will need air conditioning. Do these units have any?"

"The four units on the ends have window units. Will that work for you?" He pointed to the ends.

I looked over at Lucy, who nodded. "I think that would be fine."

"Well I'm sure you would want one of these facing the drive," he asked, looking over at us.

"Actually," Lucy spoke up, "how about one on the other side?"

"Well sure, let's have a look." He started walking around the corner.

We followed him. My guess was he could tell we wanted privacy, and best of all, he asked no questions. Dan was right; this was a good place for our needs.

Jake opened the door to the unit on the other side, which slid up rather easily. The grass that ran close to this side, looked as if it had not been cut for some time, months perhaps. There were no neighbours in sight. Lucy and I glanced inside while Jake turned on the air conditioner unit.

It was about the same size as my spare bedroom where we had the lab set up.

"It's perfect," I exclaimed. "How much do you want for it?"

"One hundred dollars a month," he replied.

At first, I thought that was high but given our need for privacy and lack of intruding questions, I said, "We'll take it."

I whipped out a wad of cash and counted out six hundred dollars. I gave it to him, hoping not to have to fill out a bunch of paperwork. He smiled and put the money in his shirt pocket.

"It's all yours," he said.

"Great, we will be back later to put some items inside," I confirmed.

"You can put a lock on the handle," he said pointing to where there was a place for a lock.

We shook hands again, and then headed back to the car. Jake closed the shed door and went back inside his house. I had not noticed any locks on any of the other doors and assumed none of them were taken.

"Well, what do you think?" I asked Lucy, as we were leaving.

"It's perfect," she said.

We drove home and started dismantling the lab, putting the glass beakers and anything breakable inside cardboard boxes. The remaining things: aprons, Bunsen burners and the like, we put directly in the trunk. I had to take the legs off the metal table to fit it in the back seat of the car. Since the unit did not have a sink for cleaning our gear, we stopped at a local grocery store and bought twelve gallons of distilled water.

We then headed back to the unit and began unpacking everything. I put the air conditioner unit on and was pleasantly surprised at how cool it blew. I had never lived anywhere that used window units before and had my doubts about them, but this one certainly did a good job at keeping us cool. Regardless, it made for a long day, and we were relatively tired by the time we finished setting up the lab again.

Jake never came out to intrude or check in on us, which was reassuring. Lucy and I speculated about who he was and his past. It helped pass the time quickly, and we both made up some lavish and sordid stories about him; each of us trying to outdo the other one's fiction. We got quite a few laughs over it.

The following day, I went over to George's house to see how the website was coming along. I did not expect too much as I assumed it took a long time to develop a website, though my idea for ours was rather plain and simple. I just wanted designs that helped to sell our product, not overwhelm people with splendid graphics. Though all of that sounded easy enough, I really had no idea how long it would take or what to expect from George. I had been told that learning to code was like learning a second language, and given my age now, I did not deem that obtainable. It seemed to me that it was something that came easier to certain people, as music does to others. Either you have the capacity to learn coding or you don't, and I did not have it.

George answered the door as usual, with Cassie right in tow behind him. She was wagging her tail excitedly as usual, and they welcomed me in. Everything looked in place except I could see the table in his back room full of papers surrounding his laptop computer.

"Let me show you what I have got so far," he said hurriedly.

I followed him into the back room. This time there was no whiskey glass lying around, only papers with notes on them. I could tell he had been working hard and seemed engrossed in what he was doing. We both sat down, and he began to explain his progress.

"I registered the website onto the dark web only, but it can be found through Torch, a Tor search engine." He turned the laptop in my direction to show me what he was talking about and then continued. "You will be able to enter through the back door of the site. I will show you the steps."

He typed some commands into his computer, and suddenly the site appeared. I was impressed. It looked clean, and although nothing was listed yet, I could see the layout.

"Oh wow, that looks good," I said.

"By getting in through here, you can upload photos. You can also type in the description of what you are selling, and it will show up in Mandarin Chinese first, then English." He seemed very enthusiastic.

"What about payments?" I asked.

"Well, since you said there are no other sellers and only one buyer, I made sure there was no hold, so you will have immediate access."

"Excellent," I said. "Now, the only method of payment we will take on this site is Bitcoin, so every price needs to reflect the Bitcoin amount. How will I be able to transfer the payments to my Bitstamp account?"

"I can make that all possible through the backdoor of the site, but I will need to know your account information."

I thought about this for a second. I was a little reluctant to let him have this information as what would prevent him from siphoning off any or all my money? I equated that to a new-found music star that unknowingly let his trusted manager squander all his wealth and fortune away.

George must have sensed my hesitation. "Don't worry; you will be able to create your own password to get onto the site, which will be encrypted."

"Okay," I agreed.

I retrieved my Bitstamp account information for him from my phone app. He inputted it all onto the site's operational board, and rather quickly at that. I was impressed with how easy he made it look.

"I've called the site Moon Lee as you requested," he said. "All of the descriptions of the site are in Chinese as well, and I registered the domain in Wuhan," he confirmed.

"Well that's good," I said, remembering my recent setback online.

"Now usually, you could keep track of which users are visiting the site, but since you are set up on the Tor browser and your visitors will be as well, you won't be able to do that. That provides them, as well as you, anonymity."

"Understood," I said.

"Go ahead and type in here your encrypted password so only you can have access to it. I'd recommend not sharing it with anyone else, and don't write it down somewhere describing it as your special password, if you catch my drift." He seemed very intent on that explanation, understandably so.

I typed it into the secure backdoor twice for verification. I made it decidedly easy, typing MoOnLeE. I did that for two reasons; to make it easy to remember and to trick anyone who might try to hack the site, such as the Feds. Knowing how they would think, they would try a million combinations that were complicated and intricate, never guessing it was the actual name of the website. Besides, it was encrypted anyway.

After I finished, I slid his laptop back over to him. "All set."

He typed a few more things in and then said, "There you have it." He slid the computer back over.

I was happy with what I saw. He took the time to explain uploading pictures and typing in the item descriptions. Afterwards, I gladly gave him another envelope with ten thousand dollars in it. I figured it would pay for itself once we got our first batch sold online. He did not count it, but really appreciated the gesture. I was glad to give it to him.

After I finished there, I drove to Wal-Mart. I decided now was as good a time as any to be safer by disguising my digital footprints, so to speak. I purchased a prepaid credit card there, putting five hundred dollars on it, using cash of course. I wanted to use that for now on when purchasing the ingredients that I needed.

I went home and jumped on the computer to purchase items for the next batch, eager to get started. Unfortunately, when I tried to order the NPP, our main ingredient, I ran into a roadblock. The order would not complete, and I was referred to customer service. I called the phone number listed and gave the lady my order requisition number. She put me on hold for a moment and then transferred me to a supervisor.

"Good afternoon, sir," the man said. "I understand you are trying to order N-phenethyl-piperidone today, is that correct?"

"Yes, that is," I said plainly.

"Well, I do apologise for any inconvenience, given you are a repeat customer sir, but there is now a government restriction on this particular item. It can only be shipped to places of businesses, not home addresses. The address on your account is flagging residential; do you have another address you can provide us?"

I quickly tried to recover from the shock of this inquiry, "No, not at the moment. My supervisor has all shipments sent to that particular address. I will have to check with him if that is okay?"

"Yes sir, that will be fine. I will put the order on hold for the time being until we can complete it."

"Thank you," I said, trying to sound appreciative, but feeling rather annoyed.

I knew if I tried any other chemical suppliers, I would run into the same issue. I stood there in the living room, cell phone in my hand, trying to figure out what I could do. It seemed daunting to me, trying to figure out how to get around this obstacle, then it struck me, Natural Weed Killer! They ran a legitimate business from their home, and I had seen them have a couple of barrels of chemicals delivered to them there. The question was if they would let me order what I needed using their address. Secondly, was it a good idea?

I already had three of my neighbours involved in this adventure of mine, not to mention that they all lived on my block. This would make a fourth neighbour. I thought about asking Dan his opinion, but I knew he would think it was a bad idea. I resolved myself to just going down to their house and asking about their weed killing product; just take it from there.

I meandered on down the road, past George's house, then Dan's and Josh's. I came up to the house just beyond

Dan's. It was a two-story home, which was not very common in this neighbourhood. Whoever built it, made it look like a log cabin in the front, with a large octagon window on the second floor overlooking the street. The rest of the house looked normal for the area, and I could tell someone in the household liked surfing, as the mailbox out front had an old surfboard cemented down on either side of it.

A young guy in his late twenties was rolling a cart loaded with about twenty FedEx boxes out toward the end of the driveway. He was not bad looking, tall with dark wavy hair. He did not seem to be in any kind of a hurry, taking his time with the cart.

"Busy day it looks like," I said to him, as I approached the house.

He nodded and smiled suspiciously at me, probably wondering why some stranger was approaching the house.

"I'm Paul. I live just up the road and was curious about your weed killer."

He looked back toward the garage area and yelled, "Dad."

A lean man about my age peaked out from around a stack of boxes lined along one side of the garage. He came out and walked down towards us, and the younger man went up to the house. I did not take offense to his lack of conversation with me and chalked it up to him just being a bit shy.

"Hello, I'm Tom and that was my son Tyler." He extended his arm and we shook hands. "He isn't one for conversation, but he is a hard worker." He patted his hand on the cart of boxes that his son had brought out.

"It looks like business is going well," I said.

"Yes, we sell everything from our online store, then pack and ship right from our home." He seemed proud of his accomplishments.

"Tell me about your product, I was thinking of buying a bottle to try along my driveway." I tried to sound as sincere as possible.

"Gladly," he said. "Come up here" and he motioned for me to follow him up the driveway.

I could tell they did most of the packaging in their garage. There were numerous boxes filled with empty plastic spray bottles. He must have ordered them in bulk. I could see the barrels of chemicals resting toward the back end of the garage. Apparently, he mixed it with water as there was tubing that ran from the barrels to a large sink. There was a spigot that had a valve device attached to the end of it, which connected the tubing from the barrel to a wider tube leading to a large plastic container. This had a red twist valve at the bottom of it from where I am sure they filled the spray bottles up.

"This is our base of operation where we fill our orders. What kind of weeds do you have growing at your place?" he asked.

"Oh, mostly loose pockets of dollar weed sprouting up from the cracks in the driveway and such."

"Well, our product would definitely take care of that. It is all natural and non-toxic, working especially great here in Florida." He began to strike me as a QVC salesman.

I glanced over to the two barrels at the back of the garage. "All natural?" I asked doubtfully.

He seemed to retreat a little defensively and said, "Well that's a naturally occurring compound that I can only purchase from a third-party distributor."

"I've seen the truck dropping those off at your house," I said, trying not to sound too obtrusive.

He walked over to a table where he had the already filled bottles, I'm guessing to draw my attention away from the barrels. "Here, try out a bottle for free and see if it works on those pesky weeds you are having issues with."

"Thank you." I tried to look excessively grateful. "Say, is your business an LLC?"

"Yes, we filed several years ago. Sales have been climbing ever since."

"Well, the reason I ask is I also make a product, but I can't afford the rent where I'm at, so unfortunately I have to shut down."

"Oh, that is very unfortunate," he said.

"Yes, it is. I was going to keep producing the arthritis ointment and sell it on the internet, much like you, but they will only ship the chemicals to a business address. Would it be too much to ask if I could have them shipped to your location here? My ingredients only come in litre-sized bottles, so it would not take up much space, and I can walk right down and get them once they arrive. It would be a great help." I felt slightly ashamed for fibbing, but I needed the NPP to continue.

"Oh man, don't think twice about it, I would be glad to help. My son is home most of the time and can sign for anything that comes here." He smiled happily.

"Thank you, Tom, that is very gracious of you," and I shook his hand.

He gave me a business card with his name and address on it. We parted and I walked back to my house, spray bottle in hand. When I got back home, I called the chemical company back and asked for the supervisor. I got the same guy I had spoken with earlier.

"Yes, I spoke with my supervisor and he said it was quite alright to ship to the business address."

"That is great sir. Can I have the business name and address?" He did not seem to have any doubts about my intentions.

I gave him the company name and address, which was on the same street as my home. "It is an LLC," I told him.

"One moment, sir," he said. I could hear him typing on his computer. "Okay sir, everything checks out. We can ship this out tomorrow."

He seemed most accommodating and I am sure he was happy to make the sale. I ordered another large quantity again in case any further restrictions were put in place. I used the prepaid credit card for payment.

It was a big hurdle to jump over, but I was able to get past it. I felt like celebrating and rushed into the bedroom to tell Lucy the good news. She had been on her phone talking with her mother. She had destroyed the other phone the Russians had given her for work to prevent them from finding her and now only used her own private phone. She looked up at me from the bed and could tell I was excited about something.

"What's up with you," she asked.

"I was finally able to order a big supply of NPP today."

I had kept her in the loop regarding all the difficulty I was having with it. I had also told her about the website George had designed for us so we could continue selling our product online. She looked extremely happy.

"Oh, that is great darling," she said.

"We can cook a large batch next weekend!" I was excited about the prospect.

She flashed me a seductive glance and then turned onto her back. She leaned back against the pillows and opened her legs, suggesting I come over to her. It occurred to me that she only rewarded me this way whenever our money potential increased, but I did not care. I was too infatuated at that moment. She continued to look at me, waving her legs open and shut. I tried to stand next to the bed, watching her for as long as I could, but it was futile. I took off my clothes as quickly as I could and then jumped onto the bed with her. I began to take her clothes off, and we began to make love. It was perfect.

Chapter 13

60 Minutes

The following Thursday, I was home relaxing after work. Lucy had ordered pizza and we were both sitting on the couch waiting for it to be delivered. It had been a long busy day and I was looking forward to chilling out that evening. We both heard a knock on the door, and I jumped up to answer it.

"The pizza is here," I exclaimed.

I could mentally smell it. Lucy knew I liked the meat lovers, and so she would order a half Mexican, half meat lover's pizza for us. I could picture dipping my slice into the garlic butter sauce, delicious. To my surprise when I opened the door, I saw Tyler standing there.

"Hey, your stuff came in today. Want to come and get it?" he asked.

"Yeah, let me get my shoes on," I told him.

He waited for me just outside the door as I got my shoes on. I was disappointed that it wasn't the pizza, but glad to be getting the NPP. I smiled at Lucy and headed out to walk with Tyler.

"I know what you're making with it," he said as we walked down to his house.

I glanced over at him. He did not seem threatening in any way. I considered playing dumb, but I was sure that would only serve to irritate him.

"Did you tell your father?" I asked, not looking over to him, but just continuing to walk unfazed.

"No, I did not," he confirmed.

He did not ask for anything: money or a bribe. I kept a cool head and continued walking with him to his house, and then up the driveway. Tyler had several of my boxes lined up just inside the garage door. I had ordered more than usual, so there were six in total.

"Could you help me carry some of these back to my place?" I asked him.

We each grabbed three boxes carefully, and then walked back to my house. On the way, I thought of what Tyler wanted from me to keep his silence. He was young, in his twenties, and though he did not seem to want for anything, I concluded that money was the best option.

When we got to my house, I said "You can put those down out here. I'll be back in just a second."

I didn't want him to feel threatened, so I left him outside with my supply of NPP. I went in and Lucy was eating a slice of pizza, which had come while I was down at Tyler's. I went back to my room and grabbed a ten-thousand-dollar stack of twenties, then went back outside to where Tyler was standing.

"For your discretion," I said, giving him the stack of money.

"Appreciate it," he said and then turned and went back up the street towards his house.

I watched him, curious to see if he would stop and count it, but he did not. I left it at that, for what else could I do? If he wanted something else later, I would deal with it then. I brought in the boxes and left them by the front door. We were going to need to put them in the car and take everything out to the storage area when we made our next batch.

Lucy and I picked Friday to cook it. We had all our ingredients, along with several gallons of distilled water to rinse the beakers in between the various steps of the process. We had seen a water hose outside of the storage unit, but not wanting to chance contaminating our product, we bought the distilled water instead.

We pulled into the storage area, driving slowly so as not to break any of the bottles of NPP on the bumpy gravel driveway. We had kept them in the boxes they were shipped in, and each litre bottle was encased in Styrofoam, but the last thing we wanted to do was take a chance of breaking one by driving too fast. Getting as close to the units as we could so Jake would have little chance of seeing what we were taking into the place, we unpacked and began our cook. Although we were cautious and quiet, we never saw or heard from Jake. Either he was busy inside his house doing something or he just did not take any interest in what we were doing, which was just fine with us. He kept to himself, just as Dan had said he would.

Despite our best efforts to remember everything, we had forgotten the heat lamp. As I was feeling tired by the time we finished, Lucy dropped me off back at the house, got the heat lamp and went back to keep an eye on everything while the powder dried. I was glad we had completed another cook but was wondering if it would be as easy to sell it online, given our site would not be as popular as the one we had been using before. I had told Lucy that our website was up and ready to list the next batch, but I had not shown it to her yet. She still seemed confident that we would have no problem selling anything, so I kept a positive outlook on things.

Before she had returned, I got a call from Dan saying he had some news regarding Igor, so I walked down to see him. I knocked and he let me in. We both sat at his small dining table. He looked as if he hadn't slept for a long while with his eyes drooping, but then again, he always looked that way.

"Just a couple of things; our good friend Josh told me the FBI is handing the case back over to the sheriff's office, which is good news," he informed me.

I looked at him intently. "Okay, so what's the bad news?"

"Your man was part of the Russian mob. Now the investigation is going to say he overdosed, but there were no drugs found in the car, not even paraphernalia. It is believed there is a war taking place between the Russian mob and the Mexican cartel. Are you and that girl you are with waging some kind of vendetta or something?" He asked, staring back at me with a concerned look.

"No Dan, nothing like that at all." I didn't want to go into detail about how Lucy and I had met, feeling a little ashamed of the situation.

"Are you at all worried about some form of retaliation from the Russians? If they were able to find you, how easy would it be for someone else to?"

I honestly hadn't given that any thought. "That is a fair point; I'll have to ask my partner about that."

"Well clearly it is none of my business, but just how well do you know her?"

I thought about this for a moment, then said, "I don't even know her last name." I shook my head in disbelief at myself.

"Can you get hold of her driver's license?" he suggested.

"I haven't seen one, but I can look. Come to think of it, I've never seen her use a credit card. She always keeps her cut in cash, no bank account." I replied, pondering how this was something I had wondered about before now, but assumed it was just to keep her safe from the IRS.

"Well, see what you can find and get back to me," he advised, standing up and walking me to the door. "By the way, *60 Minutes* is running a story tomorrow night you should watch."

I looked at him with curiosity because I had always enjoyed watching that show. "Oh yeah, what about?"

He patted me on the back and said, "Just watch it."

*

Hailey had always been a sweet young lady. She had a petite frame with long dark hair. Her smile was contagious, and everyone she met liked her immediately. She had grown up in an upper middle-class home with a lovely family. Her parents provided her and her younger brother with a very comfortable upbringing. She had done well in school, and her parents were prepared to pay for all her expenses once she entered college. But in her senior year of high school, a friend introduced her to Percocet at a party. She fell in love with the feeling it gave her, and after that, it was all downhill from there. She had the means to purchase the pain killers, making up stories to her parents about fundraising events and projects at school. But her grades began to slip, and her study time turned into time pursuing drugs.

Then one night, a random boy who attended a local college nearby whom she met at a party introduced her to syringes, and using them to inject oxycodone instead of swallowing the pills or even snorting them, which she did at times. Coming from a well-off family, she had associated intravenous drug use with homeless people: the decrepit dregs of society. But this boy was so good looking and smart. He assured her that using a syringe was the best way to get to a level of high she never thought possible. He had such dreamy blue eyes; she didn't care that it went against her best judgment; she trusted him. He dissolved a Dilaudid tablet and showed her how to inject it into her arm. He was right, she had never felt so warm and loved as she did just then.

As time went by, her use became more and more expensive. Her parents became suspicious, and tried to control her coming and going, but to no avail. As with any family dealing with addiction, friction began to build from within. The right thing to do became an arguable subject, welling up emotional feuds and cracking the foundations of stability. Her parents would argue, and her younger brother felt as if he did not exist, since Hailey became the focus of their attention.

As time went by, her use spiraled out of control. Then as the Drug Enforcement Agency (DEA) began to regulate opiate prescription drugs more rigorously, she had to switch to heroin. The DEA, a government run entity, halted the flow of opiates to pharmacies across America by requiring them to dispense a much higher ratio of non-narcotic prescriptions to their customers. A drug wholesaler kept track of the purchase orders, and restricted existing pharmacies from ordering large quantities of opiates. New pharmacies opening up were restricted from ordering pain pills altogether for sometimes a one-year period, preventing them from servicing customers who were in need. This left the nation's population struggling to find their prescription painkillers, including cancer patients. A large percentage had to resort to using street drugs. Counseling and rehabilitation were an afterthought, implemented far too late in the war on drugs.

So, Hailey became another statistic. She left home and dropped out of school. She had not so much become embarrassed about her use; more she had become enslaved to it. She became indebted to several dealers, and that is how she fell into service for the Russians. They kept her housed and supplied with a reliable source of drugs, and in return she had to perform sexual favors to certain clients. It was not the life she had planned for herself, but at least she did not have to expend so much energy in search of her next fix.

Once Lucy had gotten her out of their grip, her habit still lingered. So, she still resorted to life as a call girl to help support herself, only now Lucy was her supplier. This suited Hailey just fine as Lucy seemed nicer and only checked in with them once a week. She did miss living at the house though, as the motel was grungy and cramped. She sometimes yearned to go on long walks, but there was not much for her to see where they were located now.

Around six o'clock, she got a call from what seemed to be a nice gentleman. He wanted a dinner date for a couple of hours and would pay whatever was required in cash. This was not uncommon, as men sometimes just wanted company to go out and eat with. They enjoyed having conversations; some complained about their wives or jobs, others were just lonely. She would enjoy the dinner and then would get paid for it as well, so she gladly accepted the opportunity. She arranged to meet the man at the front of the motel at eight o'clock. She was glad she wouldn't have to eat take-out tonight, which was the norm since there was no kitchen in the motel.

Hailey got dressed and let the girls know she had a dinner date. A few minutes before eight o'clock, she went around to the front of the motel to wait. Soon, a black

Cadillac CTS pulled up, which was not a very common car for this area.

The gentleman inside rolled down the front passenger window and asked, "Blue?"

Blue was the name she went by online to advertise her services. Since their main form of advertisement was shut down, she figured he must have gotten her number from a friend. She leaned down to look into the car. The man was in his thirties and was very good looking.

"I sure am, handsome," she replied and got into the front seat next to him.

She saw that he was very well dressed, with a black sports jacket on and slacks. He looked tall and was well groomed. She wondered why someone so good looking would need to hire a girl for a date. He pulled out onto the interstate and headed south toward Port St Lucie. He drove carefully and was in no rush.

"So where are we going?" she asked to break the silence.

He smiled and kept on driving. She looked at the dashboard panel and was impressed with the lights and buttons. She figured he was shy and wondered how she could get him to talk.

"Is this a business dinner or a social outing?" she kindly persisted.

He smiled again and then said "Well, that depends."

"Depends on what?" she asked, smiling back.

"You'll see."

He continued driving, then exited off the interstate to Saint Lucie West. It was fairly dark outside now being in the winter, the days growing shorter, but she recognised the area. He calmly drove up to the gate of the neighbourhood where she had lived with Dimitri and the other girls. The guard did not even come out, just opened the gate for them to drive on through.

Hailey felt panic stricken. She was frozen in her seat and didn't even try to open up her door; she couldn't. The man did not say anything, just continued driving to Dimitri's house. Several other nice cars were there, and the man parked behind them at the end of the driveway. Hailey sat dead still and did not speak a word. He got out of the car and serenely walked around to open her door. He put his hand forward to help her out of the car, which she took hold of, and then they walked up to the house. He was not at all rough with her, which in its strange way, terrified her more than if he had been. Opening the front door for her, they walked in together. Inside were two other men and a tall woman talking in the living room. The house looked the same as when she had left; nothing seemed out of place. The three people stopped talking as they approached. Hailey was guided over to the recliner, where she sat down after checking that it was okay to do so.

Her escort said, "This is Blue." He went over to the long couch by the others and sat down, crossing his legs, and keeping an eye on her. His cool demeanor was chilling, and Hailey kept her eyes on him. The other two men went and stood behind the couch so that they were all facing her from across the room. None of them spoke, but the man who brought her there for some reason looked more comfortable than the other two. Sitting on the couch, Hailey instinctively figured he was their superior. What she did not know was that he was the younger lover of the woman standing in the room, which thereby gave him a very high status. She was the highest-ranking person of the Russian syndicate on the eastern coast, including New York. Her power was absolute, and her orders never questioned. She enjoyed her lover's company not so much for his good looks as for his lethality. Although he was quiet by nature, he had never failed at eliminating any obstacles that were required to be removed. He had a meticulous nature to him as well, patient, and observant. He was also the woman's personal bodyguard. What neither one was aware of was the fact that she had ordered the death of Lucy's father, a Mexican drug kingpin. This had proven very difficult for the Russians, and it was almost thought of being impossible to achieve, but when Lucy's father visited Miami, they were able to execute him. What they did not count on was his daughter seeking retribution.

The woman slowly walked towards Hailey. She was holding a glass with a small amount of scotch in it. She was taller than the average woman, with a slender yet healthy physique. She was a confident looking woman who was used to giving orders. She wore Tory Burch sandals and white trousers, with a vest shirt that was buttoned just enough to see she was not wearing a bra. She was rather striking and had an air of sophistication about her.

"My name is Katrina," she said with a Russian accent. "Do you know why you are here?" she asked Hailey.

Hailey was terrified and shook her head.

"You are here tonight because of the strange disappearance of our good friend Dimitri. We already know Igor was deliberately killed. Did you know this?" Katrina asked again.

Hailey shook her head, too frightened to speak.

"Of course, you don't." Katrina stood tall next to Hailey sitting in the chair. "Where is Dimitri," she asked intently.

"I don't know ma'am," Hailey answered nervously.

Katrina circled slowly around the living room, running her finger in a circle around the top of her glass. She walked behind the couch where the two men were standing, then back to where Hailey sat. Ivan continued to sit on the couch, legs crossed, staring at her. Katrina kneeled close to Hailey at the side of the chair.

"Ivan tells me he picked you up at the Motel 6 in Fort Pierce. Is that where your friends are staying also?"

"Yes ma'am, all except for Lucy." Hailey began to cry.

"And how have you been getting your 'supplies?'"

"Lucy brings it to us every week." Hailey could not stop sobbing now; she felt so intimidated by her current surroundings.

Katrina stood back up and glanced toward Ivan. He reached over to the glass coffee table in front of him and picked up what looked like a small wooden cigar box. Opening it, he pulled out a syringe.

"And this Lucy, where does she stay?" She looked down at Hailey expecting a sincere answer.

"I don't know ma'am. We think she has a boyfriend but none of us have met him." She was being truthful. The girls speculated on Lucy's whereabouts and assumed, correctly, that she was with the man whom she had spent so much time with prior to disappearing.

Ivan approached holding the syringe in his hand. Katrina looked at him and gave him a nod. The other two men continued to stand off behind the couch.

Continuing to sob, Hailey said, "Please ma'am, I don't want to die. I'll come back to stay here. I promise."

Katrina knelt beside her again. She put her drink down on the floor and held Hailey's hand. "I believe you."

Ivan quickly injected the needle into the side of Hailey's neck, right into her artery. She tried to turn her head and neck away, but it was already too late. She felt the familiar warmth she would encounter when using, but then she lapsed into a listless sleep.

"Go ahead and finish her," Katrina politely ordered him.

Ivan went behind the chair and wrapped his arms around Hailey's neck, like a wrestler would do a sleeper hold on an opponent. Once Hailey stopped breathing, he released his arms. He stood up and looked at Katrina.

Katrina spoke to him intently. "I want to create a little unrest in the beehive. We need to draw out the queen bee. I want you to dump Hailey here back at the hotel. Leave no trace that you were there; then I want you to bring me this Lucy."

Ivan nodded and then went to the kitchen to grab a knife. Katrina looked at the other two men who had continued to stand behind the couch. "You two will take over operations here at this house once we get this Lucy."

They both nodded and said, "Yes ma'am."

*

The next evening, Lucy and I made a batch of popcorn and sat down on the couch to watch *60 Minutes*. We had just finished listing our latest batch onto the new website, which George had made conveniently easy for us. Lucy was most impressed. She liked the name of the site and the whole concept of it misleadingly originating from China. We entered the description and just as George had said, it listed it first in Chinese, then English. We had the one bulk batch, and I still had my doubts about someone being able to afford buying it all at one time, but Lucy insisted I'd have faith. By the time we finished our listing, the show was starting, and we were ready to relax for the evening. But after seeing what the lead off story was, "Online Overdose," I felt myself getting tense.

I turned and looked at Lucy, "Well, this is gonna be fun."

She frowned at me, understandably so and said, "How nice of Dan to recommend this for us to watch."

We sat through the special, which reported on the flood of opioids online, specifically fentanyl, and how this drug was creating a drastic rise of overdoses across the country. It was presumed that drug cartels were using fentanyl to increase the potency of heroin and thereby creating a higher demand for their product. But it was leaving a wake of deaths due to overdoses when opiate naïve people would use it for the first time. Even addicts who had been using for some time would overdose by craving more and more, using the drug excessively, thereby leading to their ultimate demise. It was a very compelling story to say the least. They also addressed the influx of the drug and concluded that most of it came from clandestine labs like ours or was being synthesised in China and shipped here. Since different labs were making it, the potency of the drug varied as well. This made using a game of Russian roulette for addicts. Cities across America were scrambling to get a foothold on the situation.

I became deeply disturbed by what I heard, but Lucy seemed unmoved by the programme, and afterwards, started playing Sonic the Hedgehog on her phone. Then, out of the blue, she said, "Let's check the website and see if it sold."

"Oh, there's no way," I said with certainty.

She looked at me with gleaming eyes, so I opened the laptop and took a look. "Well what do you know?" she said triumphantly. She did not seem that surprised.

I looked and to my disbelief, the shipping address was the same as the buyer who had purchased from us before. "Look at that," and I pointed it out to Lucy.

"They must have searched online and found our new site," she said, shrugging it off.

That night, despite the good news, I hardly slept. Lying in bed, I thought of all the deaths I might be responsible for. It made me feel uneasy to say the least. I also wondered if perhaps the seizure of the site we had chosen initially, was timed to happen just before this story aired on television. Law enforcement always seemed to have a funny way of looking effective at the most opportune times. Be that as it may, my morals were tugging at me hard. Lucy, on the other hand, slept like a baby. I sat up and stared at her. How could such a nefarious creature look like such an angel?

Chapter 14

Smoke on the Water

The next morning, I awoke to a chilly and overcast, almost dreary day. The wind was dead calm, but the cold air was thick. I felt as if I were still dreaming as I had not slept well. I stood out in the living room staring out of the window with my coffee in hand, waiting for that familiar caffeine jolt to hit me. Across the way, on the lake, there was a mist of fog hovering over the water. It seemed to move slowly across, putting me in a trance. Once it reached the edge of the lake, it evaporated so that there was only the fog over the water, nowhere else. The warmth of the water compared to the colder air must have produced it.

"Cool," Lucy said, walking up to me and looking out the window. "Smoke on the water," she commented, and she began to hum the notes to the song.

I continued looking out of the window and felt slightly annoyed.

Sensing I was contemplating something, she said, "Come on, let's walk over."

She did not bother to put a jacket on and opened the front door. I could feel the chill creep in, so I left my coffee on the windowsill and followed her out. We walked over to the lake, Lucy getting there quicker than me. I strolled, putting my hands in my front pockets to try and keep them warm. She squatted down beside the lake and observed the fog, rolling somewhat aimlessly from off the water.

As I approached, she said, "Now, tell me what is bothering you."

"I'm starting to think we should stop making the stuff. You know, I make great money at my job, a lot more than most people. Besides, I'm beginning to feel guilty about what we are doing. Who knows what innocent people are dying because of our product?"

She stood up and looked out onto the lake, then walked up to the very edge of the water. "Think of all the life that exists in this lake; tadpoles, fish, turtles and even water snakes. Everything depends on one another; feeds off each other. It's a community of coexisting creatures, not so different than our world, our community. People provide needs and services to others around them; it's how we survive. Lawyers, doctors, mechanics, postal workers all provide us with a need or want. What we provide is a want, a pleasurable one."

I was impressed with her analogy. "Yes, but what we make is killing people," I reminded her.

"Honey, if we don't make it, someone else will. There will always be a demand." She seemed to have delivered that rather curtly.

I resented her for saying that as it had nothing to do with the moral aspect of what I was saying. "You know, I don't even know who you are, I mean who you really are."

She looked at me scornfully. "What do you mean by that? I've given myself to you, given you my body!" She began to walk in a circle, looking down at the ground as she walked near me. She seemed distressed.

"Yes, you have, and I appreciate that, I really do. But we haven't even told each other 'I love you' yet." I was beginning to feel frustrated inside, wondering how the conversation drifted to this. She held onto her silence. "I mean, I'm not even sure if I know your real name."

I guess I was looking for a connection with her on a deeper, mental, even an emotional level. It felt as if there was this hidden wall between us, a barrier of sorts, which kept us from truly sharing our feelings with each other. I had been chalking it up to the fact that we met through a business arrangement: her providing for services paid. But as time progressed, and we seemed to have grown closer, at least physically, I desperately wanted to be closer mentally. It just was not being reciprocated.

"What is it you want to know? Do I love you?" She glared at me rather coldly.

"Well do you?" I asked.

"I care about you very much," she replied.

I felt somewhat let down and confused, even used. "I killed a man for you," I blurted out.

"I never asked you to do that," she retorted.

"Now you see, it's that kind of vacant response that irritates the shit out of me," I said, exasperated.

"Do you want me to move out," she asked.

I couldn't believe she asked that, so effortlessly, as if she were going out to get some groceries or something, except to not come back. It was a callous question, and I felt exposed. Of course, I let my pride dictate what I said next, "Do what you feel you must."

"Well can you drop me off near the Motel 6 on your way to work?" she said, angry and annoyed.

"Sure, no problem," I said defiantly.

I felt somewhat defeated. It seemed odd that she was so capable of ending things between us with such ease. I chalked it up to our age difference, a generation gap between us, I assumed. Whatever the reason, I felt like I missed something, and it went right over my head.

We walked back over to the house and she packed her belongings while I showered and got ready for work. I was surprised at how little she had accumulated over the last few months. She certainly travelled light. I grabbed the keys and we both got into the car. Sitting next to me, she had a look of being pissed off, so I did not say anything, just drove. It was about a twenty-minute drive to the motel, but it went quickly.

"I'm hungry. Can you drop me at McDonalds?" She did not look at me when she asked, only stared ahead.

"Sure, no problem," I replied, not wanting the situation to flare up any worse than it was.

I pulled into the parking lot and she got out, taking the black duffle bag of belongings that was in her lap with her. She did not look back, nor hesitate, as she went inside. I felt irritated, but, as she walked away, my eyes followed her. She always seemed to leave me in a trance of admiration. Perhaps I was just in love with her body?

All that day, I was in a cranky mood. I did not really feel like talking to anyone, and when I did, I was short and curt. I tried not to think about Lucy, but it was useless. I thought about our conversation and the way the events unfolded. I felt somewhat cheated by how easily she walked away from everything. It was as if it made no difference to her if she were with me or not. I was upset with myself for developing feelings for her. She was obviously too young for me. That didn't seem to be an issue for her. When we were together, intimately, it felt amazing. It was more than just sex, it was something deeper, or so I thought anyway.

During my lunch, Sarah came into the break room to check on me. "Say, everything okay? You seem a bit cranky today."

"Yeah, just a crappy day is all," I said, and smiled.

"Well snap out of it already!" She commanded me, smiling as she left.

She was right; there was no reason to let it ruin my day, or week for that matter. To distract myself, I stopped at an Asian market on my way home to buy a box of spices.

I planned on using the empty box to ship the fentanyl to continue the presumption that our product was from China. I did think it was quite the coincidence that the same people who were purchasing from us on the first website also found us on our new site. Was it possible that Lucy had been in contact with them and informed them of our new website? Her mother lived in Miami after all.

In any case, I decided to shut down the whole operation. I did not want to be responsible for anyone's death undeservedly. Besides, after all the recent expenses, and the loss of the last sale to the FBI, I really was not that far ahead. Everything just seemed to be more of a hassle than a reward.

I dropped by Dan's house to tell him what I had decided. I parked out in front of his yard and walked up to the door. As soon as I knocked, he opened the door.

"Hey, I just wanted to drop by and tell you I was quitting the business."

"Good, I'm glad to hear it," he said. "What about your lady friend, is she on board with it?"

"Well, to be honest, she moved out this morning." I hadn't planned on telling him about that.

"Ah ha," he replied with a sort of sly demeanor. "Well, did you ever get her name and driver's license number?" he asked.

"No, I did not. Does it really matter now?" I replied although I didn't really want to think about her at the moment.

"No, I guess not. Just be careful," he warned me. "I'm a little worried about you."

"Thanks," I said and looking at him, I could see he was genuinely concerned.

"You remind me of my late son. His life was snatched away from him way too early, and I don't want to see the same thing happen to you."

"Oh, I'm sorry to hear that. I promise I'll be careful."

He looked at me intently, but in his eyes, I could see doubt. I patted him on his shoulder and smiled, then headed to my car to leave. He stood at his doorway watching as I drove to my house.

I cooked dinner and ate. Afterward I sat down at the table in my back porch with a glass of whiskey. Dan was right. I should know more about Lucy than I did. I decided to go through all the dresser drawers in our room and the storage bins in the spare bedroom. Getting up, I poured myself another drink and then went searching. I found nothing in our drawers, but in the storage bin where she had kept her money, I found a handgun and two cell phones. The phones were the same make, and I guessed that they belonged to Dimitri and Igor. But why would she keep them I wondered.

I took the batteries out of each phone so they would lose power. I then smashed the phones with a hammer. I took the broken pieces and their batteries over to the lake and threw them into the water. The last thing I needed was for someone to track the phone's location. I went back into the house and poured yet another drink. It helped warm me up and to think clearer. I decided to hide the gun up on the shelf in my bedroom closet. That way, it was out of site, yet close enough to make me feel safe, just in case.

I felt mentally exhausted. Though it was somewhat early, I laid down onto my bed. Alone for the first time in a while, I was able to relax. The past few months felt like a blur, and I just wanted to put it all behind me. A vacation, that is what I needed. The thought of Jamaica came to mind.

Even though I lived in Florida, near a beach, there was a vibe there that I had never seen or experienced anywhere else. Everyone there was so laid back and friendly. "No worries man" was the phrase of the day, each and every day. I had been there once with Tricia, back when we were dating and happy. We had a blast, and I had longed to go back there ever since. I closed my eyes and thought of the beaches there, putting myself in a peaceful, nirvana place. It was like I was catching my breath for the first time in a long while.

Just as I was drifting to sleep, my cell phone rang and woke me up. It was Lucy, and when I answered, she was crying.

"They killed Hailey," she said, all upset. "Can you come get me?"

Chapter 15

Happy Meal

Lucy wanted me to pick her up at the McDonalds where I had dropped her off earlier. I found myself torn inside about going to get her. Part of me was excited to see her, whereas the other part was reluctant to go. This created a bit of a nervous tension within, part exhilaration and part nauseousness. If I had to admit it, Lucy had this drawl that kept me longing for more. Being educated, I knew I should not be involved with her. She was nothing but trouble, but I didn't care. There was something inside of me that overrode all sensibility; any common sense I possessed. This something made me rush out to see her again, despite my better judgment. I got in my car and drove out there.

When I parked at McDonalds, I could see the flashing blue lights of a police car parked next door at the motel. Instead of going inside the restaurant, I let my curiosity get the better of me. I meandered on over to have a look at what was going on. It looked like a typical crime scene that you see on television, with the yellow tape surrounding a body covered with a white sheet. There were a couple of plain clothes detectives taking notes, standing near the body, and Josh! He was taking pictures and had what looked like a red, plastic toolbox beside him. His crime scene van was parked close by alongside the cop car which had its lights on. I didn't really want him to see me, so I hesitated to get any closer, but it was too late. He glanced over in my direction and spotted me. He did not wave, nor motion to me, but merely nodded at me and then continued photographing.

Lucy had not told me much about what happened. All she said was "they" had killed Hailey and that was it. Her body lay in the motel parking lot just outside of the office. Apparently, whoever "they" were, they wanted her body to be easily found. Even though there were a few other stragglers observing, I did not want to linger too long. I went back over to McDonalds and sat inside. It took a while for Lucy to show up, but when she did, she had her duffle bag with her. She sat next to me and placed her bag on top of the table.

Hugging me, she said "Thanks for coming to get me."

She looked happy to see me, and the fact that I had dropped her off here this morning due to our argument did not seem to matter to me anymore. I was glad to have her back safe and sound. I waited anxiously for her to tell me what happened.

An older black lady, who looked frail but had a face of wisdom, was slowly walking by us. She saw us sitting together, side by side and commented, "You two make a sweet couple."

"Thank you, ma'am," I replied.

Her eyes smiled as she looked at us. "How long have you two been together?" she asked.

"Six months now," I said, smiling.

"Well God bless you, goodnight," she said and slowly walked out.

We both chuckled. "Aww, do you hear that babe, we make a cute couple," I said sarcastically.

She grinned and said, "You're such a dork."

"Are you hungry?" I asked.

"A little, yes," she replied.

I got up and went around the corner to order us some food. Looking at the menu, I decided to order us a couple of happy meals, just to be a smart ass with apple wedges for her and cookies for me as our extra choices. I paid and waited a few minutes for them. Once they had our meals ready, I walked back to the table and sat back down next to Lucy. She smirked precariously and we started to eat.

"So, who killed Hailey?" I asked while biting into a cheeseburger.

"Her name is Katrina, and we are going to have to kill her." She said this so calmly and with precision that it almost put chills down my spine.

"Ah, I don't think I signed up for that," I said.

"Look, you wanted to know who I am, right? Well now I'm telling you. This woman had my father killed, and now she won't stop until we are both dead. She is a cold and calculated killer. I took a chance when I left there because I liked you, but this is something I have to see through to the end. Are you with me on this or not?"

"You told me your father passed away last year," I said inquisitively.

"Yes, he did. He was shot to death in Miami." She became visibly upset when she said this.

"Oh shit, I'm sorry. And it was this Katrina? Why would this woman want him killed?" I asked.

"Does it matter?" She looked annoyed, but knew I needed some answers. "When you killed Dimitri for me, I thought that was so sweet of you. I also saw that as a chance to save the other girls, so I moved them out of the house we had been staying in and put them up here at the motel. I figured that would be the last they would have to deal with the Russians, but they must have had Hailey's contact details. The girls told me she had left last night to go on a dinner date with a client, and that she never came back."

I noticed she had shifted the attention back over to Hailey and away from her father. I followed suit, "Tell me how we can avenge Hailey's death."

"I'm not sure you should get any more involved than you already are," she said.

"Well what about your friends? Are they safe staying here at this motel? I would hate for something else bad to happen," I told her.

"Oh, I moved two of them to another hotel and one is taking a Greyhound bus back home to Orlando. All of them got rid of their phones." She seemed very calculated.

"Thank goodness for that," I said. "Well I'll be your protector and keep you safe." I gleamed at her with a big smile.

She chuckled. "Come on then my big stud, let me show you how much I appreciate you."

She got up and led me out to the car holding my hand. Even though I was extremely nervous about the Russian mob coming to kill us, all I could think of was my immediate gratification and sleeping with Lucy. All that other stuff would take care of itself, for now anyway.

*

Ivan sat in his car across the street from the Motel 6. Being a T&A parking lot, it was a busy plaza with lots of semi-trucks coming and going. There was a CAT Weigh scale station as well as a long stretch of diesel bays for truckers to fuel up in. There were a few fast food restaurants inside as well as a shop and showers for the over the road truckers.

Over the last couple of nights, he had been observing the motel across the street. Concentrating primarily on the coming and goings of the girls, he noticed they resided in the last three rooms around the back. They did not go out much except for food. The night before, he saw two of the girls walk over after dark to the truck parking lot working as 'lot lizards'.

Despite his good appearance, which was somewhat contrary to the area, he had a natural ability to blend in unnoticed. Perhaps it was his quiet demeanor that helped. He was never bothered by anyone given his look not of meanness, but of someone who had inflicted pain and fear in people before, without thinking twice about it. This he would do undaunted by any potential legal circumstances; he transcended any of that. He did have very kind eyes, which always seemed to put women who he came across in a trance of sorts. He also dressed well, usually in black slacks with Christian Louboutin shoes and Brioni jackets. This always turned a kind eye from most women he came across, which was a useful characteristic at times in his line of work. None of that mattered to him romantically though as his loyalty was for Katrina, who was his female equal, especially with regard to killing.

Tonight, once he had dropped Hailey's body off after dark, his main objective was to find Lucy and bring her back to Katrina. His patience always seemed to reward him. His favorite quote, which was on his screensaver, was 'Beware the Fury of a Patient Man.' He had seen her walk over to the motel from McDonalds earlier, but being it was daylight, he wanted to wait until dark to nab her. Then he caught sight of her leaving the motel and walking back over to McDonalds. He took out his binoculars from the glove box and focused in on her. Being the police were close by, investigating Hailey's death, he had to remain patient. But it did have the effect he wanted; it brought her back out from the motel. He followed her with the binoculars and saw she sat down next to a man. He observed them talking and then eating together. From the looks of it, he guessed that they were a couple. He saw an old black woman stop by their table and say something before leaving.

At first, he was tempted to call Katrina and let her know he would be bringing Lucy to her sometime tonight, but he did not do so. He didn't know anything about the man Lucy was with and so he stayed on the side of caution for now. As they got up and went out to a car, Ivan started up his Cadillac. He followed them carefully so as not to be noticed by them. They left downtown and headed north. He thought they may drive into a gated community, which would hinder him from following them, but they did not. Instead, it was a neighbourhood with no guards. He kept his distance, as it was starting to get late and there were fewer cars out on the road. Finally, after several turns, they pulled into a driveway of a house that was across from a small lake. On one side of the house there was a lot filled with trees and heavy shrubbery. He decided to park across from the lot so he could get an unobstructed view of the house, while remaining unseen from anyone inside.

The wind blew cold from across the lake, making it feel colder where he was located. The rustling of tree branches and leaves made him that much more camouflaged, as any noise he might possibly make would be concealed by the sounds of nature around him.

He watched them go into the house, and a light went on in one of the rooms, which looked like it was a bedroom window. It was the only light on, and he remained in the car, scanning over the house. No other lights came on, so he figured they were in the same room together. After about an hour, the light turned off. The whole house was now dark inside. He waited another hour, to give them time to fall asleep, then got out of his car. He donned his black leather gloves and then quietly opened his trunk and took out a small kit he used to unlock doors. There were no people out and about and no cars on the roads. He stealthily walked over to the front door to gain access to the house and to retrieve Lucy.

*

A noise startled me awake. It sounded like it came from out in the living room, so I sat up in bed. As it was windy outside, I figured it was something that landed on top of the roof. While sitting up, I roused Lucy awake.

"What's going on," she asked half awake.

Before I could answer, a man walked into our room. He was holding what looked like a gun, but it was hard to make out what it was since it was dark. A flurry of chills came over me. The man turned on the bedroom light and pointed the gun at us.

He scanned over the room and then looking at Lucy said, "You're coming with me." I looked over at Lucy. "We don't have any use for you," he said, as he moved the gun in my direction.

I said the first thing that came to my head. "Are you here for the money?"

I tried to remain calm, as calm as one could, sitting naked with a gun pointed at them. My heart raced but I tried not to show it. I just sat still, not making any sudden moves.

Lucy played right along with me without hesitating, "Shut up Paul, he doesn't know anything about it!"

I looked at her scornfully, "Well what the hell else would he be here for? Is he an ex-boyfriend?"

She slapped me across the face, which was instantaneous and caught me by surprise.

"What is this money you are talking about?" he asked in a light Russian accent.

I looked at him squarely in the face, "It's in the closet," and I pointed forward. I slowly got out of bed, looking completely harmless being naked, and walked up to the closet door. Lucy remained dead calm with her breasts exposed, sitting in bed. The man came close behind me with his gun still pointed at me, but not too close given my lack of clothing. I slowly opened the door and reached up onto the upper shelf where I had hidden the gun I found earlier in the day. I felt for it and then put my hand around the handle.

Lucy yelled, "Don't you dare give him our money!"

He turned halfway around to her, "Shut up."

I picked up the gun from the closet and pointed it at his head while his attention was on her and fired. It was a loud, piercing sound and my face was splattered with skull fragments and blood. His body immediately fell to the floor near the base of the bed. Blood and brain matter lined the walls around me; it was a bloody mess.

I looked at Lucy, somewhat dumbfounded. "How many more of these guys are going to come for you?"

"I'm sorry babe. He must have followed us here from the motel. Hey, where did you get the gun?"

I sighed, "I don't want to talk about it right now."

"Okay," she said, and then slid out of bed and started getting dressed.

I dropped the gun onto the man's back and stepped over his body. For some reason, this second murder I had just committed did not seem to affect me like Dimitri's. Either I was becoming a hardened criminal, or I was just too tired to feel anything. All I knew was that I needed a shower. I had that drowsy feeling still lingering despite all that just occurred, and I wanted to clear my head. The last thing I wanted to do was make a bad decision right now. I knew I was going to have to call Dan; I just did not want to be lectured by him. Not that he would do that, it wasn't his style. It was his 'I told you so' stare that I was dreading.

After taking a long, very hot shower, I got dried off. I slowly walked back into the bedroom while drying my hair off with a towel. Lucy had gotten dressed and was doing her best to contain the blood flow. I also got dressed and then called Dan's cell.

When he picked up, I said, "Sorry for the late call but I've got a problem over here and need your help."

"Okay," he replied slowly, "I'll be over soon."

I turned on a few more lights in the house so it would not look so dark and ominous inside, though it felt like it was. About fifteen minutes rolled by before Dan came knocking at the door. I opened it up and let him in. He walked by me without saying anything and I directed him to the bedroom.

He glanced at Lucy and then said, "We are going to have to get rid of him quickly. Where is his cell?"

I looked over at Lucy, who shrugged her shoulders. Dan went over to the body, careful to avoid stepping in any blood. He patted the man down, getting his wallet and keys.

"Okay," he said. "I take it that's his car parked across the street. We are going to put his body in the trunk. Paul, if you would please move your car out of the driveway so I can back his car in, that would be appreciated."

He headed out and I quickly followed to move my car out of the way. He put on a pair of gloves and got into the Cadillac, backing it all the way into the driveway. He then walked up the street towards his house.

While he was gone, I asked Lucy, "So, where is his cell phone?"

She gave me a stern look, stating, "This won't be over until I kill Katrina."

"Why?" I asked becoming frustrated. "Why did they murder your father?"

"I don't want to talk about it right now," she answered.

"When do you want to talk about it?" I said trying to pressurise her.

Just then, Dan knocked on the front door again. I gave Lucy a piercing glare, then went to let Dan back in. He had opened the trunk of the Cadillac and was carrying a blue tarp. We wrapped the body up carefully as his head was caved inward from the bullet. We carried it outside and quickly placed it in the trunk of the car.

Dan shut the trunk and said, "I'm gonna need you to follow me out to the salvage yard on Angle Road, and you're gonna need to bring ten thousand dollars."

"Understood," I said. "When did you want to go?"

"Now, we need to go now," he said very firmly.

"But it's still dark out. They're not going to be open yet," I said perplexed.

"I know the owner; he's gonna meet us there. And besides, you need to get rid of this car and all of its contents ASAP." He went and sat in the Cadillac.

I went inside and grabbed the money and my keys. Lucy was in the bathroom taking a shower. I figured Dan would not want her to tag along with us, so I left without saying where I was going. I got into my car and followed Dan once he pulled out. It was that time of night when all the late-night partiers were dead asleep and the early morning workers were just getting up. It was pitch dark and windy. Aside from an occasional semi-truck, no other cars were on the road.

We got to the scrap yard in good time. It was a large complex with just a dirt road leading up to the main gate. It was not well lit from the outside. A man whom I presumed was the owner was standing by the gate, and when we got there, he opened it. Dan drove on in and the man waved me in as well. He was tall but chubby and was balding. Once we were inside, he closed and locked the gate.

I parked just within and got out, bringing the money with me. The yard was much larger than I had imagined. There was a scale set up just inside for people who were selling scrap metal or aluminum to drive up onto. Beyond that were rows upon rows of cars that had been in bad accidents. Many of them were missing parts as well. There were also stacks of rubber tires throughout the yard.

Dan had driven the Cadillac up to a crane that had a four-pronged clutch used to pick up vehicles. It was further back in the yard, near a very large and deep metal dumpster of sorts. That was the metal compactor. It was well lit back there as there were several large cement posts with spotlights beaming from them. I followed the owner back to that part of the yard. Dan got out and greeted the man, then stood back by me as the owner walked onto a wooden platform next to the dumpster. He pushed a round green button and the compactor started churning. He then got into the crane and cranked it up, using it to lift the car. He punctured the windows out in the process, and then placed it inside the compactor. As I stood next to Dan, we watched silently. We could hear the metal crunching and glass shattering. It was impressive to say the least. I felt like I did when watching a bonfire at night, mesmerised.

The owner shut off the crane and then walked over to us. "All set gentlemen," he said.

"I appreciate the favor John," Dan said, then he glanced over at me.

I gave John the stack of money and he said, "Thank you, sir."

We began to walk back towards the front gate. "Will it sit here long," Dan asked.

"No sir, I have a truck coming to drive several of these up to New York later today, including your Cadillac."

"Good deal. Thanks again," and Dan shook John's hand.

Dan and I got into my car and John opened the gate far enough for us to get out. Once we were clear, he closed the gate back up. My eyes were burning from being so tired. Dan must have noticed.

"You want to grab a cup of coffee at the Waffle House?" he asked.

"Sure, why not," I said.

So, I drove us out there. It was just off the interstate, and the morning traffic was just beginning to pick up pace. The dawn was breaking, and we could hear the cars racing to their destinations. I had felt heavy and tired while sitting in the car and it was an effort to get myself up out of the seat. We went inside and sat at a booth. The windows were sweaty with condensation. There was only one waitress and a cook who stood behind the counter.

"Two coffees please," I said to the waitress when she came over.

"Would you like something to eat?" she asked.

I looked over at Dan who was sitting across from me and he shook his head. "No thank you, just coffee."

I felt relieved to be rid of that problem. The waitress came and poured us both a cup of coffee. I proceeded to make a little pile of empty sugar packets and cups of half and half while stirring them into my coffee. Dan drank his black.

"So, is this going to become a regular event?" he asked.

I gave him a tired, discerned look. I stirred the half and half and sugar into the coffee so it would blend in better. I imagined the man's body blending into the crushed vehicle while being compacted. I thought I saw my coffee turning red, as I thought of his body becoming mangled with the metal of the car. I slowly took a gulp to try and wake my brain up.

Dan continued. "It's really none of my business kid, but I would advise you not to go to war with the Russian mob." He took another sip of his coffee. "You don't strike me as the violent type. Are you in over your head?"

I looked down at my coffee and started stirring it again. "I don't know yet."

He gave a deep sigh and grunted "ah hmm."

"Can I ask you something?" I said.

"Go ahead," he said curiously.

"How is it that several of the neighbours on our block seem to have no issue dealing with illegal matters? It seems a little too convenient to me."

"Yeah, I figured you'd start to wonder about that."

I looked at him with intrigue.

"We all worked for the same gentleman I had told you about when we first met in one capacity or another. He helped purchase the homes for us on the same block so we could keep an eye on each other, so to speak."

"And that is how you knew Josh would help me out with the blood stains," I said, seeing the clearer picture.

"Correct," Dan confirmed.

"You said he was eventually murdered?" I wondered if Dan had anything to do with it.

He looked at me uneasy and said, "Your coffee is getting cold."

Chapter 16

To Steal from the Dead

I called in sick from work that morning. I was way too tired to go into a job that required one hundred percent of my concentration. Then, there was the mess in my bedroom that needed to be cleaned up. I also wanted to find out why the Russian mob murdered Lucy's father, if that was, in fact, true. I found it mildly frustrating how she would only divulge bits and pieces of major information about herself. It was like chasing after breadcrumbs in a detective novel. Sharing was clearly not her strong point to be sure, and whenever I would pry, she withdrew or got angry.

I dropped Dan off at his house and went home. Getting out of the car, the sun felt warm on my face. It had been a long chilly night. I went inside and looked for Lucy, hoping not to get into another argument.

"Honey, I'm home," I yelled sarcastically.

She came out from the back of the house. "Hey hey."

"We got everything taken care of, thank goodness."

"Oh, that's a relief. Hey, did you want to order more ingredients from the proceeds from our last batch?" she asked.

"Ah, I don't know if I want to keep doing it anymore to be honest with you."

"Boo," she replied. "Who doesn't like making money?"

"I hear ya, but I'm a little concerned about the fact that what we are making could be contributing to the deaths of people we don't even know. I do have a conscience."

"It's not wrong to steal from the dead you know," she said bluntly.

"What do you mean?"

She came over and sat down next to me on the couch. She took a relaxed posture toward me and put her hand on my shoulder. "Those people just wanted to numb their feelings to the world around them. They did not want to be a part of society, they wanted to separate themselves from it. They were dead to the world already. So, if they wanted to spend their money on what we make to help them do that, where is the wrong in that?"

I could not think of an argument against that statement, so I asked her about something else. "What about these Russians who keep showing up to the house? I understand that you want vengeance for your dad, but I want to be able to sleep peacefully at night. I don't want to have to keep looking over my shoulder every time I go outside either. This incident last night was way too close; we might not be so lucky next time."

"Yeah, I'm sorry about that. I'm going to fix that problem real soon, don't worry," she assured me.

"Oh yeah, how are you going to do that?" I asked, trying not to sound sarcastic.

"Don't you worry about it. This will all be taken care of soon. Now, I know what you need."

She got up and took hold of my hand, leading me into the bathroom. She started to undress me and then turned the shower on. The steam began to roll out of the open shower door and fog up the mirror. She undressed and went in the shower, making it look ever so inviting. She picked up a bar of soap and then used her pointer finger to motion for me to join her. I went in smiling and closed the glass door behind me. She began to wash me in circular motions with the soap, first on my chest, then lower and lower. The hot water beat against the back of my head and ran down my back. As the soap began to lather up the front of my body, she moved forward and rubbed her body up against mine. She then stepped back and leaned against the shower wall, looking at me with seductive eyes. We were both drenched in water. I went toward her and slid myself into her. We made love standing up with the hot water beating upon both of us. It was so seductive that I came quickly. Afterwards, I felt as if all the tension in my body had melted away.

"That was fucking amazing," I said, somewhat drained.

"Good, now go get some rest. I'll be there shortly," she said with a loving smile.

I grabbed a towel and got dried off in the room. I was too tired to get dressed and just laid down in bed naked. She stayed in the shower a bit longer and got cleaned up. A deep chill sank into my weary bones as I thought about the last twenty-four hours. Who is this girl, and why did it feel like she was pulling me into something I didn't want to be a part of? I felt like I was losing control of everything. I needed to know who Lucy was, but I had no idea how to find out. Then it suddenly occurred to me that if I had a picture of her, perhaps I could discover exactly who she was.

I jumped off the bed and grabbed my cell phone before she got out of the bathroom. I trotted back into the room and lay back down on the bed. She came out drying her hair with a towel. I patted my hand lightly on the bed for her to come next to me.

"Haven't you had enough," she asked me.

"Come here," I said seductively.

She wrapped her hair up with the towel and sat on the edge of the bed. I slid up next to her. She looked at me suspiciously.

"Let's take a selfie together; I want to remember this day forever."

I tried not to sound like I had an agenda. I just made out as if I was infatuated with the moment. I put the camera on in my phone and then pointed it at us. The lighting was good since it was daylight out. We both smiled and I snapped just one picture. We both looked at it to see how it came out. It was a good picture and it looked clear.

"Don't post that online anywhere," she warned me.

"I won't," I said, and smiled. "So, who are you?"

"I'm whoever you want me to be," she replied.

"That's reassuring," I said, half asleep.

It felt good to lay there on my stomach, naked with the air conditioner gently blowing on me. I badly needed some sleep. I closed my eyes and forgot about the mess that was on the wall behind me. Before I knew it, I was asleep, peacefully oblivious.

*

Lucy got off the bed and got dressed. She quietly went outside to have a cigarette and then came back inside. She got out her cell phone and dialled apprehensively, waiting for an answer.

"Yes," a man answered.

"It's Lucinda."

"Yes ma'am. How goes it up there?"

"I will be shipping out the fentanyl today." Lucy lit yet another cigarette.

"Good. Does the chemist suspect anything?"

"No, he is happy." She glanced back toward the hallway to the bedrooms to make sure no one was there.

"Where do we stand with the Russians," the man asked.

"Well, we just killed their 'sweeper'. He was intimate with Katrina. Once she finds out about it, she will come back up this way, and that will give me the opportunity I need to kill her. Once that is accomplished, we will have strict control over the drug trade here in Florida."

"Good, I like the sound of that. What are your plans for the chemist?"

Lucy paused for a second. "I haven't decided yet."

"He isn't part of the cartel," the man reminded her.

"I'm aware of that," she said defensively.

"Good, then you know what you need to do."

The man disconnected and Lucy rolled her eyes. "Familia!"

*

I woke up out of my long nap. Groggy, I was in a haze. I did not even know how long I had slept. I glanced over at the nightstand next to the bed and saw my cell phone was still where I had left it. I remembered the mess on the wall and turned to have a look. It was mostly wiped away thank goodness, but a lot of the area was still stained. Lucy must have cleaned it while I was asleep. It was that time of afternoon when the sun was beginning to settle in the west. Although it was still light out, the sunlight was of a gentler hue that was easier on the eyes. There seemed to be no wind out either and the day seemed ready to give way to night. I stretched and let out a weary sigh, then got dressed. I could hear the television on in the living room. I put my cell phone in my back pocket and walked out there to see Lucy sitting on the couch watching something on Netflix.

"Hey sexy," I said, seeing she was watching an episode of *Shameless*.

She looked up and smiled. "Hey hey. I got our batch packed and shipped while you were sleeping. Hope you don't mind; I didn't want to wake you."

"No, that's cool." I stood there for a second scratching my head, still trying to gather my thoughts after my long mental absence. "I need to walk down and see George about moving the Bitcoin from the site. Want to order pizza?" I asked, trying to sound inconspicuous.

"Sure, that sounds good. You must be hungry."

"I am, especially after our workout." I smiled at her wryly.

I was very hungry as I had slept all day without eating. I was feeling very unmotivated, so much so, that I did not even want to be bothered calling for take-out, so I left it in Lucy's hands to order for us. I went outside and meandered on up the road. It had warmed up considerably from the day before. The last remaining rays of sunlight casted by the orange sun felt good on my face. I was not used to going all day without being outside. Even at work, I would walk out back of the pharmacy and soak up some rays, no matter how hot it was outside. To me, it was the best way to deal with stress. No matter how bad a day I was having, just standing in the sun for a couple of minutes always seemed to calm my nerves. And so, I took my time walking down to George's house, breathing in the fresh air, listening to the birds get settled in for the dark night ahead and smelling the various dinners being cooked from around the neighbourhood.

Besides, George had already shown me how to transfer any Bitcoin deposits off the website and into my Bitstamp account. I thought about how I would ask him about Lucy's photo; how to find out exactly who she was. I figured someone who knows how to develop a website, no matter how simple it was, would also know how to find out something like that. I wracked my brain trying to figure out how to do so myself and concluded that it was easier said than done.

I got to his door and knocked. Again, Cassie barked from within, and again George answered. I felt slightly awkward not calling ahead, but he seemed happy to see me.

"Hello Paul, how are you?"

"I'm good sir," and I petted Cassie on the back. She soaked up the attention.

"Come on in," he said. "How do you like the site? Is it easy to access and use?" he asked eagerly.

"Yes, thank you, it is. I've already listed and sold an item on there." It occurred to me that he could have searched for the website himself, given he knew the name of the site, and saw what it was I was selling.

"Well that's good news, I'm glad to hear it." He seemed happy.

"Say, I have a picture of someone on my phone and wanted to find out more about the person. Do you think you could help me with that?" I hoped I did not come off as a stalker or something.

He looked at me for a second and then gave it some thought. "That's not really my area of expertise. The person you should ask is Tyler up the street. He is a tech genius."

"You mean the kid that lives with his father who sells the weed killer?" I asked surprised.

"Yes, that's him. Have you ever met him?"

"Yes actually. I'll have to go down there and ask."

"They are good people," he said reassuringly.

I wondered if Tyler was part of Dan's former crew. He walked me back to the door. I gave Cassie a quick scratch on the back of her head as she lay on the floor. Going out, I turned and headed in the direction of Tyler's house, but stopped off at Josh's house first.

He must have seen me approaching as he opened the front door before I knocked. "Hello Paul, come on in. I just brewed some coffee; do you want some?"

"Oh, no thank you."

I went on inside. Even though I slept all day, it seemed kind of late in the day to be drinking coffee. He seemed eager to have me come in and I worried about why. Given he had seen me at the motel the night before, I wondered if he was going to grill me about it. I had to remind myself that he was just a crime scene investigator and not a police detective.

His house looked even more disheveled than the last time I had been there, with books concentrated around his couch area in the living room. He came out with a cup of fresh coffee and sat down. He did not seem worried about the appearance of his house.

"I was wondering if you had some more of that solvent you had made for me previously," I said inauspiciously.

"I believe so, let me check." He quickly got up off the couch and went back to the laundry room area. After some rustling around, he came back out holding what looked like a bleach container missing its labeling. "I had made some extra just in case," he said and handed it to me.

"Thank you," I said.

"Don't mention it. Say, I remember seeing you last night at the Motel 6. Did you know the girl who got murdered?"

"No, not personally," I said, hoping not to rouse any suspicion.

"Well it was a mess. They believe she may have overdosed on heroin given she had track marks on her arms. Shame really, she was so young." He took a sip of coffee.

"That doesn't sound like she was murdered," I observed naively.

"No, but she also had all of her fingers broken, which was done post-mortem. That is not being released to the press by the way."

I looked at him inquisitively, "So someone was trying to make a statement?"

"Not trying, did." He leaned forward, "They also carved a Russian hammer and sickle on her forehead with a knife." He paused for a moment to let that sink in, and then continued. "The Feds believe there is some kind of rivalry going on around here, and that perhaps this was a response to the Russian mobster they found dead in his car last month."

He was referring to Igor. Of course, he had a pretty good inclination that I had something to do with that, but he did not press the subject. But since he saw me near the crime scene last night, he knew it was no coincidence. I didn't say anything.

"It's really none of my business; just be careful," he said thoughtfully.

"I will, thanks," I replied.

It felt like everyone was telling me that; to be careful. It was an uneasy feeling that comes over you when you have members of the Russian mob coming to your house with the sole intention of retrieving Lucy. This last gentleman, who looked very slick, said he had no use for me, only Lucy. Why was she so important, and why had they killed her father? She obviously knew more than she was telling me. I had thought we were growing closer, but now I questioned that. I was starting to get tired of living in suspicion, doubt, and fear. It was time I found out more about her.

I bid farewell to Josh and walked over to Tyler's house across the street. By this time, it had grown dark. I noticed a light on in the garage and saw his father working inside, labeling boxes to ship out to customers. I admired his ability to work from home; to be his own boss essentially, and all within the realm of being legal.

Tom had his back to me and so I walked on up the driveway to greet him. "Hey Tom, how are you?"

He turned around, slightly startled. "Oh, hello Paul." He looked down at the container I was carrying. "Did you have any success with our weed killer?"

I had not tried it out yet, but I said, "Oh yes, it's been working wonders on those pesky weeds I've been dealing with lately."

"I'm glad to hear it. Did you need some more?"

"No actually, I'm here to see if Tyler could help me with a computer issue I'm having." I tried to sound convincing.

"Well, if it has anything to do with computers, he is the one to ask. Come on in, I'll show you to his room."

I followed Tom through a side door that led us into the kitchen and dining room areas. Inside it was well lit. The house was airy and spacious with large windows in the front. They had nice furniture throughout and there was no clutter, unlike Josh's house. The floors were wood and well waxed. I noticed a large television in the living room area which was towards the back of the house.

We continued onto a hallway that led to the bedrooms. He knocked on the first door to the right and waited. I was impressed with how nice his house was.

"Yeah," Tyler yelled from within.

"Paul is here to see you," Tom said.

"Oh, let him on in."

Tom opened the door and motioned for me to go in, then went back out to the garage. I went in and closed the door behind me to maintain a sense of privacy. I was not even sure if Tyler had any company with him in there but scanning the room, I could see he did not. It was fairly dark with all the curtains shut. Light emanated from a large computer screen sitting on top of a desk and an even larger television from which he was sitting in front of playing video games. It looked like a computer nerd's den and a video gamers delight. The chair he was sitting in was a large recliner that was black. It looked very comfortable. I could tell his room had been extended into what used to be a second room, so that it took up the entire front end of the house.

His computer desk took up a large part of the back wall of the room, and the computer looked custom made. It had purple neon light bordering the panels and the hard drive case was made of glass so one could see the inside components. I had never seen a computer like that in any store. The screen was active with what looked like a chat room of some sort. Various users were typing in queries constantly.

He definitely did not go without, but despite having all these amenities, he did not strike me as being pretentious. Being young; in his twenties, he was part of the Instagram generation. He would get interested in new things that sparked his interest but would get easily bored as well if something remained constant or monotonous. As with most youth, he was quick to focus attention and just as quick to lose interest.

After taking in my surroundings, I asked "So, I was wondering if you could help me?"

"What can I do for you?" he asked back.

"I have a picture of someone, and I want to find out more about the person; who they are and what is their background, to be precise?"

"Where is the picture," he asked as he sat down at his computer.

"On my cell phone," I said.

"Let me see," he said, as he turned his chair around towards me.

I reached for my phone in my back pocket and pulled up the selfie picture of Lucy and me. I then handed over my phone to him. He looked at it for a second.

"Isn't that the girl that lives with you?" he asked.

I gave him a flat, embarrassed look.

He turned back towards his computer. "What's her name?"

"I'm not a hundred percent sure. She goes by Lucy. I know her mother lives in Miami and that they are of some Spanish descent, perhaps Mexican." I suddenly realised just how little I really knew about her.

"Okay," he said. He forwarded the picture to an email address from my phone. Then he opened the email from his computer and pasted the picture onto his screen. He then edited the selfie, so it was just her face, leaving mine out of it.

I was impressed with just how fast he was able to accomplish all of this. He then opened a drawer and pulled out a tiny notebook with website addresses and browser names. Just inside the drawer I noticed the stack of money I had given him from before, untouched. He turned and gave me my cell phone back.

"I'll run her image through a facial recognition programme. I should have something for you in a couple of days at most," he said, as he started typing rather quickly on the computer.

"Okay, thank you," I responded, rather impressed.

He noticed the jug I had been given by Josh. "Are you going to be ordering more of your compounds?"

"I haven't decided yet. I'm thinking of quitting that business."

He did not seem to care one way or the other about my response. He seemed rather absorbed in his new task. My guess was he enjoyed a challenge. Not looking at it so much as a job or work, he probably challenged himself to find out as quickly as he could who Lucy was. Not so much for my safety but plainly out of curiosity. I picked up the jug and let myself out of the room, closing the door behind me. I left the same way Tom had led me in. On my way out of the garage, I bid Tom goodnight and headed back to the house to begin the arduous task of cleaning up the room.

I found that the pizza had already been delivered when I got there. Lucy and I ate together, and afterward I was tempted to go back to sleep, but I wanted the room cleaned up as the site of the shooting was rather chilling. It then occurred to me that since we had been together, we had not gone out on one date publicly. No photo identifications, no bank accounts, and no public showings. I began to feel anxious for what Tyler would find out for me.

*

Tyler double checked what he saw on his computer screen before getting up. He was usually of a calm demeanor, but this made him nervous. He walked down to Dan's home just a couple of houses away and then knocked on his door.

Dan opened the door and waved him inside. "Tyler, what did you find out?"

Tyler went and sat down at a small dining room table just inside. He had been here plenty of times before and felt comfortable enough to do so. He looked at Dan with a worried face. "Well, it's not good. She is the head of a Mexican drug cartel."

Dan went and sat across from him. He could sense Tyler's apprehension. "Okay, relax. Tell me everything you found out."

"Her name is Lucienda Cortez from the Cortez cartel. You're familiar with them I imagine?"

"Yeah, I'm familiar with them," Dan confirmed.

"She's been staying just up the road from us at our friend Paul's house." Tyler gave Dan a concerned look.

Dan thought about this for a few moments. "Well that explains the turf war happening here with the Russians."

"Do you think Paul knows who she is?" Tyler asked.

"Oh, I doubt it. Go ahead and make Paul aware of it and see what kind of reaction you get." Dan got up from his chair. "I'll get the others ready. I know where the Russians will be staying. I know Paul might not like it, but we will need to kill her; it's the best thing for him. We've worked too hard to get the heat off us and the last thing we need is a turf war in our backyard. We take care of this tonight."

And with that, Tyler got up to leave. He knew what Dan meant by that and what was going to happen. He started to walk up to Paul's house to give him the news.

Chapter 17

Sinnerman

The next evening, after I had returned home from work, I got a knock on the front door. Lucy and I were planning on discussing what to do with the money we had just made, and I was relieved to have a distraction from that subject. I looked out of the living room window cautiously and saw Tyler standing outside.

"Oh, it's Tyler," I said with some relief.

I opened the door and he said, "Hey man, I have that bottle of weed killer you ordered if you would like to come get it." He stayed where he was, not seeming to want to come inside.

"Oh yes," I said, playing along. I turned to Lucy. "I'm gonna walk down and get this real quick. I'll be back in a few."

"Okay," she said.

I could tell she was anxious to order more ingredients, but I, on the other hand, was not. This was good timing on Tyler's part, not that he planned for it to be. I was certainly curious to see what he found out about Lucy.

I went out and followed Tyler, who walked rather quickly, back to his house. I found it a little hard to keep up with him given his fast pace, which seemed to put a sense of urgency on the situation. I followed him into his house and straight into his room. I did not notice Tom anywhere.

He closed the bedroom door behind me. "Why didn't you tell me your girlfriend was a member of the Mexican drug cartel?" he asked, sounding a bit irritated.

"Ah, because I didn't know," I said bluntly.

He walked over to his computer screen and pointed. It was showing the FBI's top one hundred most wanted list. I looked and saw Lucy's picture on it.

"Well you were right about her first name, somewhat. She is Lucienda Cortez of the Cortez drug cartel. She's number eighty-six there," and he pointed at the screen.

"What the fuck," I said, dumbfounded. I looked closer at the screen to make sure it was her and sure enough, it was. It was not a mug shot of her, and I was curious as to how they came upon a photo of her. It was not from the selfie I had taken of us together, but it looked fairly recent.

"What is she wanted for?" I asked, somewhat afraid of what I would hear.

"Drug and human trafficking, money laundering, tax evasion and murder," he said in a very matter of fact and precise way.

I frowned and said, "Well that's wonderful."

"Yeah, I bet. You really didn't know?" He seemed surprised by that fact.

"No, I didn't," I confirmed.

"Well, I did some research on her. Her father ran cocaine into Miami for a couple of decades. Then he got into human trafficking, smuggling immigrants up from Guatemala and Mexico to the States. He also started smuggling heroin up from South America. The Russians killed him over it. It is believed she took over the operation, but then she disappeared, went off the grid, so to speak." He looked fairly concerned.

"Yeah, she mentioned that the Russians killed him."

"Ah, well, did she mention she was a member of the Cortez cartel?" he asked with skepticism.

"No, she left that part out." I was taking this in.

"Well, be careful. I'm not sure what you are into, but if you didn't know she was a member of a Mexican drug cartel, what else isn't she telling you?" He looked at me with discerning eyes.

"Got ya," I replied.

"Be sure to grab a bottle of weed killer on your way out, my dad won't mind," he urged me. "When you get back home, I don't want her to be suspicious of me in any way."

"Okay," I said.

Tyler stayed seated at his computer while I left, contemplating, and digesting everything I had just found out. His note of caution and look of concern said it all. What had I gotten myself into? I felt myself drift, to disconnect from the whole situation, to up and leave. Somewhat as I had drifted after killing Dimitri. Again, it felt as if time had stood still, that my surroundings stood motionless. I became engrossed on figuring out how to get out of my current predicament. I wanted to put as much distance between myself and Lucy as possible, but there was no easy solution. She was living, or should I say hiding, under my roof. If I let on that I knew who she was, what would be the consequences? I only imagined the worst.

Why was she intimate with me? What was all that about, and was it all a sham? I suddenly felt used; like she had taken advantage of me. I gathered that she was a cold, calculating person. Worse still, she was patient enough to draw out these Russian mobsters one at a time, until she was able to get to the one she believed was responsible for killing her father. I felt like a pawn used to distract an opponent in a game of chess. But what was the bigger picture? Was this a gang war or just vindication?

Whatever the case was, I began to miss Tricia. I hadn't heard from her for some time now, and I wondered how she was doing. I missed the warmth of her snuggles at night after making love, something I never seemed to get from Lucy. She was more likely to go and play Candy Crush and smoke a cigarette after sex than lay next to me and cuddle. When sleeping next to Tricia, if I had ever gone to use the bathroom, Tricia would suddenly wake up and ask where I was going. I was more likely to find Lucy up watching a reality television show.

For no reason, other than to reminisce, or out of just plain curiosity, I paused in Tyler's garage and pulled up Facebook. I searched Tricia's name and then tapped onto her profile. My intrigue turned to disappointment as I saw her profile picture had changed to that of her and another man. Scrolling down, I saw that she was 'in a relationship'. I scanned lower and saw several posts where they had checked in together: Disney, dinners out and even a cruise to the Caribbean together. I felt disgusted. While my life had digressed to drug trafficking and murder, she was off enjoying life in a romantic and productive manner.

It occurred to me that this all stemmed from one bad recommendation from my friend Steve and my decision to follow through on it. If I had never seriously given any thought to what he had said, I would not be in the predicament I was in now. I mean, what kind of person meets a woman who advertises sex online? What did that say about my moral integrity? I became angry with myself and my poor judgments. I was angry at how happy Tricia appeared in her posts. I charged home, mentally distraught over what I had seen.

When I got home, I found Lucy still sitting on the couch. She looked at me a little perplexed. "Where is your bottle of weed killer?"

"Oh, never mind that," I said quickly. "Tell me how we can get revenge for your father's death." I needed to get my mind off Tricia, to move forward. I felt like I had already caused so much havoc in my life, why not kill a few more people. I felt blind with rage inside.

She looked at me surprised. "That's so weird. I just took a call from Katrina a few minutes ago on her lover's phone; you know, the man that we killed. She thought she was going to talk to him but got me instead."

"Oh yeah," I said. "And what happened?" My heart pounded quickly as if I had just run a marathon.

"She was furious. She knew who I was without me even saying so. She will probably be at that house tonight planning her retribution. I figured this would be my best chance at killing her." She looked very excited, like someone who was finally reaching the completion of a long, arduous journey.

Without thinking, I said "Let's do it!"

"I never asked you to get all involved in this," she said, feeling guilty. "I feel bad entangling you in this mess already."

"I know, I know, but what the hell. Let's take care of this woman once and for all."

She looked at me inquisitively. I was shocked at my disregard for any potential consequences. My frame of mind was in an apathetic place, with no real urgency to move away from it.

"Do you still have that gun?" she asked me.

"No, we disposed of it along with the body."

"That's okay, I have a couple of guns we can use." She went to the bedroom and pulled out a couple of pistols from her bag. "They both have silencers on them as well, to keep the noise to a minimum. Obviously, you know how to use one at close range." She held them up so I could see them. "Now, the silencers will add a little extra weight to them, so you will have to concentrate on your aim." She sounded like a professional, which didn't surprise me given what I had just learned about her.

I didn't even question where she had acquired them from. I just looked at them. She handed me one and I could feel what she was talking about. I didn't care about what we were about to do, I was so incensed by Tricia's new-found love life. I felt somewhat reckless, not caring about the consequences, only living in the moment. The fact that I had so much to lose never entered my mind.

"When do you want to go?" I asked.

"Let's go tonight after it gets dark. I still have the key to the front door, so we can take her by surprise."

"Well that sounds simple enough, but do you have a plan?"

"Sure, we park at the gas station, walk into the development, quietly let ourselves in the front door and shoot every person inside." She seemed very nonchalant about it.

To my surprise, I became anxious to get started. I felt trapped, like a caged tiger, and just wanted to go. I had this sense of urgency to keep moving so I wouldn't pick up my phone and look at Tricia's profile again. Lucy could tell something was up and probably chalked it up to nervousness.

"Try to relax," she said, and she gently got the gun from me and along with hers, put them inside her purse. "Come sit over here," she told me.

She pointed to the couch, and we both sat down and put the television on. She put Netflix on, and we watched a couple of episodes of *Nurse Jackie*. It was hard for me to concentrate, and time seemed to drag by very slowly.

Finally, around ten o'clock, she said, "Come on, let's go."

She picked up her purse and we went out to the car. It was quiet out, and like a bank robber who was having second thoughts just before going in, I became nervous. The one thing that made me feel confident to go on was the fact that Lucy was a hardened criminal already, that this was nothing new to her, so I felt somewhat protected. She certainly was no novice to violent acts.

I pulled out of the driveway slowly and headed in the direction of our destination. "I want to thank you for coming with me to do this," she said.

I smiled and kept on driving. We kept quiet the rest of the way towards Port Saint Lucie. I kept a slow but steady pace, not wanting to get pulled over by the police for speeding. We finally got to the gas station and parked. Since it was late, not as many people were there as in the daytime, but it was still open, except for the barbeque diner.

We got out and started walking towards the development. My heart began racing as we walked past the guard house and down the sidewalk. She had a look of serious intent on her face and I could barely recognise her. As we passed under a streetlamp, I noticed her eyes, dark with anger, gleaming forward. She was a woman on a mission, and I dared not say a word so as not to distract her.

After a couple minutes of steady walking, we turned into a driveway that had three luxury cars parked in it. There were no people outside. We walked up to the front door and she took out a set of keys from her purse. She also took out the guns, handing me one of them. It felt heavier than I remembered it from earlier. I used both hands to hold onto it, putting my finger on the trigger, ready to go. She ever so quietly, unlocked and opened the door, and away inside we went, me following closely behind her.

Next, everything happened so quickly, like a scene from a movie. We walked past the kitchen and into a nice living room, where a tall blonde lady was standing holding a drink. She was yelling at two big men dressed in black suits sitting on a couch. The men were facing us, and Lucy, without hesitation, shot each of them twice in the chest. The woman turned, surprised at what just happened, but not spilling a drop of her drink. She had a stern look on her face, looking at Lucy with a cold stare. She seemed unphased, like she was no stranger to violence. I walked over to the other side of the living room behind the couch where the two dead men sat and pointed my gun at the woman.

"You know this was only business," she said to Lucy in a reserved Russian accent.

"You made it personal when you killed my father," Lucy replied, then she looked at me. "Paul, meet Katrina, the woman who had my father murdered." Lucy held her gun up to the woman's forehead.

"Killing me won't solve anything." Katrina looked over at me and then continued. "Does he even know who you are?"

Lucy remained quiet. Katrina turned towards me and took a sip of her drink while Lucy continued to hold the gun at her head. I stiffened up a bit and my gun felt very heavy.

"She is no better than me. She poisons you Americans with drugs, uses her own countrymen to mule it into the States, and murders anyone who gets in her way."

Lucy cocked her gun.

Katrina took another sip of her drink and then said, "Get on with it already." She kept looking at me so as not to see what Lucy was about to do.

Lucy shot her point blank in the back of the head and Katrina collapsed onto the floor. The glass she was holding toppled with her, with the ice clinking out. She looked far less lethal laying on the floor, lifeless, than she did just moments before.

I had continued to hold my gun up, not wishing to move for some reason. It was now pointing at Lucy, who was still standing on the other side of the couch. I realised I had not fired a single shot, whereas Lucy had fired five times. She still had one shot remaining. She looked at me cockeyed, turning her head slightly, wondering why my gun was still pointing in her general direction.

I sighed, "She's right you know. You're no better than she was. I know who you are Lucienda Cortez, I know."

"These people killed my father and forced my mother to go into hiding for fear of her life." She then lifted her gun up and pointed it at me. "Oh Paul, Paul, Paul; you were someone that was in the right place at the wrong time."

I knew the last shot was meant for me. I lowered my gun down to my side. "Did I ever mean anything to you?" I asked.

"You are someone I will never forget," she said kind of cryptically.

"Remember Lucy, that tomorrow you can look at yesterday."

I took one last look at her and closed my eyes. My thoughts ran back to the first time I had seen her, and I remembered how sexy she looked; how infatuated I became with her. Perhaps I offered her a brief escape of sorts from the troubles this world gave her. I figured that if I was going to be shot by someone, it might as well be her. Why not? I had made too many bad decisions recently that probably took many lives, if not all at once and quickly, then certainly slowly and painfully. I waited for my destiny. Life really is not hard to manage if you have nothing to lose.

Just then I heard a shot fired, but it had come from directly behind me. I opened my eyes and saw Lucy lying on the floor beside Katrina. Dan walked out from behind me; from the dark hallway that led to the back bedrooms. He looked at me and then went over to where Lucy and Katrina both lay. He placed the gun he had shot Lucy with into the right hand of Katrina and fired a bullet into the wall near the kitchen.

Dan then looked over at me. "I'm gonna need you to give your gun to Josh."

Josh then came out of the back hallway behind me wearing black leather gloves like Dan's. He came up to me and held out his hand. I handed him the gun I was holding that Lucy had given me, and he wiped it down. He then went and put it in Dimitri's room. When he came back out, he started rummaging through Lucy's purse.

"How did you guys find me?" I asked, amazed that they were there.

Then Tyler came out with a small electronic device checking for hidden cameras and recorders. He found one inside a picture frame and put it inside a black duffle bag he was carrying, alongside a laptop he had found in one of the rooms. He did not say anything, just quietly scanned throughout the house.

"We've been keeping an eye on you now for some time, and Tyler there was able to ping your phone when you lent it to him last night. You need to get out of here now, kid," Dan said to me, "and don't ever look back."

"How did you know we were coming here?" I asked him.

He looked over towards Tyler, then said, "Don't worry about any of that. I just don't want you to ever mention to anyone what happened here tonight, you understand me?"

"I understand," I said, nodding. "Thank you, guys."

They all nodded back at me in appreciation. Josh followed me up to the door and opened it for me, then shut it closed as I left. I found myself retracing my steps back without even a glance upward. I did, however, notice George inside the guard house. He was taking the recording disks out of the recorders and placing them in a plastic bag. He waved at me as I walked by. Waving back, I quickly walked back to the car. I felt like I was given a reprisal, and I did not want to waste it.

I cautiously drove back to Fort Pierce and out to the storage unit. It was pitch black out there, given Jake did not have any lights in the area. I could see a television was on in his house. I walked quietly to the storage unit we had rented and opened it up. Once inside, I turned on the light and began to dismantle the gear we had. I was surprised by how little it took to create a clandestine lab. Most of it consisted of glass beakers of various sizes. Those I placed in a large garbage bag and then shattered them to pieces. I also got rid of the Bunsen burners, aprons, goggles, heating lamp and scale.

When I carried the bags out to my car and opened my trunk, I found Lucy's black bag in there, filled with her belongings. Apparently, she was not planning on sticking around after killing Katrina. Not bothering to look inside, I placed it into a garbage bag of its own and tied a knot. Having gotten all the incriminating evidence from the storage unit, I drove to the back of a grocery store close by and placed all the bags in a dumpster.

By the time I got home, I was exhausted. I knew I would be in no shape to work the next few days, so I called the owner of the pharmacy and told him I had a death in the family and would need the next couple of weeks off to make arrangements and such. He was very understanding and empathetic. I then took a long, hot shower, hoping to wash away the nightmare of the last few months, but to no avail. The next best thing I could think of was some whiskey, so I sat down at my dining room table and started to drink. For some strange reason, I decided to call my friend Steve and see how he was doing.

Hello," he answered.

"Hey Steve, it's Paul. How are you, brother?"

"It's been a while. How is the new place? You haven't gotten back with that bitch, have you?" he asked.

I replied, "The house is good, but I tell you man, it has been a long, strenuous few months." I finished my drink and poured some more whiskey into the glass.

"It sounds to me like you need a vacation, you know, a little rest and relaxation. You remember how good of a time you had in Jamaica, don't you? You should go there," Steve suggested.

"That is a good idea Steve, I may just do that," I concurred.

It did sound like a good idea. I jumped online and booked a flight leaving West Palm Beach at nine o'clock the following the morning. I stayed up all night, excited at the idea of getting away for a while. I also booked a room at the Sandal's Resort, sparing no expense. I wanted to spend as much of the money I could from the sale of the last batch we had made, spending it on something I would truly enjoy.

The next morning, I found myself on an almost empty flight over, being it was the middle of the week. I sat at a window seat so I could stare out over the ocean. We flew low enough for me to see the color of the Atlantic change from a light green to a deep blue. I began to wonder why Dan and the others on my block were so willing to help me. He said they had all worked for the same man before, doing whatever was needed. He made it clear to me that this person was involved in criminal activity. I also wondered if Dan had killed him. Perhaps their employer had something to do with the death of Dan's son he had mentioned to me. But that didn't explain why they helped me last night. Dan did say I reminded him of his son, so perhaps he did not want me to succumb to any danger. All of these thoughts swirled around in my head and I began to feel dizzy. It was then that I noticed the color of the ocean below change back to a turquoise green. Little deserted islands began to appear, first sporadically, then quite frequently. The plane began to descend lower and I could see the islands grow in size and contain more vegetation. I quickly forgot about the previous night's events and fixed my gaze onto the scenic islands below. It wasn't much longer until we landed in Jamaica. Once I passed through customs, which did not take long, since I only had two carry-on bags, I found a taxi outside.

"A light traveler," the taxi driver said to me in a thick Jamaican accent. "Where to man?"

"The nearest beach," I said, and smiled.

"No worries man," he said, smiling back.

After twenty minutes, we pulled up to a private beach area that had a beautiful sandy shoreline with several lounge chairs. It was perfect. I reached into my shorts and pulled out a wad of money.

"Here you go sir," I said, as I gave him a fifty-dollar bill.

"Thank you, man. I'll wait right here for you," he said, looking excitedly at the money.

"Oh, you don't have to do that," I said, grabbing my bags.

"No worries man. Besides, it's slow today anyway." He smiled and lit up a cigarette.

I walked on up to a lounge chair and lay down. Being lightly dressed in a button-down Tommy Bahama shirt and shorts, it was not too hot for me. I took in my surroundings. There were only a few locals wandering around the beach and no tourists. The sea was calm and green, with small lisps of water encroaching onto the shore. An occasional seagull would fly over every now and then. I breathed in the salt air and sunk comfortably into the chair.

Closing my eyes, I listened to the water serenely break onto the shore and then retreat. I drifted into a deep, relaxing sleep, which lasted for what must have been a good while. I had no dreams that I could recollect, and when I did finally wake, it felt like I had been lying there for months. For a moment, I had to think about where I was and how I had gotten there. The recent past seemed like a hazy fog that I did not wish to recall.

The taxi driver to my surprise was still parked close by. He must have noticed that I had woken up since he started walking down towards me. I double checked and saw that my two bags were still next to the chair.

"I must have fallen asleep," I said to him as he approached.

"No worries man, you must have had a long night."

I thought about the last few months and all that had taken place. Was I being irresponsible taking on such risky and impulsive behaviors? My lack of restraint caught me by surprise. I wanted to analyse this in my mind but deflected it to something else, not wanting to take responsibility for it all. I concentrated on something more pressing at that moment to me, food.

"Say, I'm starving. Do you have any place around here that serves good barbeque beef brisket?"

"This is Jamaica man, we don't have any brisket here, but I can take you somewhere that makes the best jerk chicken on the island." He looked excited at the chance to show me.

I slowly picked up my two bags and said, "Lead the way, my man."

"You know, I hear a lot about CBD oil; that it's becoming really big in the States. My daughter and I grow the best ganja here in Jamaica and better than anywhere else in the world man. How do you suppose a person like me can get in on a piece of the action over there?"

"Your daughter eh?" I asked intrigued.

"Yeah man, she is the most beautiful girl in all of Jamaica!" He smiled with a father's pride.

"I'm not sure. Why don't you tell me all about it," I said, and we got into his cab. On his radio, *Sinnerman* by Nina Simone played.